The Radiant Dove

Caged in—caged in, in the old station 'growler', taking her to servitude.
Hair smoothed straitly back beneath the plain bonnet, brown cloak
over a gown of dull dove-grey. Miss Bird—Miss Jane Bird, who once
had been dressed in gay coloured silks, with flowers and feathers and
lace: who once had been petted and loved, trotting off beneath Mama's
wing to her dancing lessons, her drawing lessons, her French....

Well, the lessons would avail her now: driving off into servitude as
a governess. Passing on her way a glimpse of the sort of romance she
would surely never now know?—smiling face upturned, fair head bent
to kiss the palm of a small white hand.

Absurd that, when later that moment must be recalled, her heart
should turn over at the news that the lady concerned loved the gentleman madly: that the gentleman concerned was a fortune-hunting
rake.

Miss Bird—whom her pupil christened, on account of those quiet
browns and greys 'Miss Dove'. But who went to a ball, like Cinderella,
in a shimmering dress, and came to be called by all her small world
'Miss Radiant Dove'.

Whom romance didn't pass by, after all.

Caged in – caged in, in the old station
'growler', taking her to servitude. Hair
smoothed straitly back beneath the
plain bonnet, brown cloak over a
gown of dull dove-grey. Miss Bird –
Miss Jane Bird, who once had been
dressed in gay coloured silks, with
flowers and feathers and lace: who
once had been petted and loved,
trotting off beneath Mama's wing to
her dancing lessons, her drawing
lessons, her French . . .

Well, the lessons would avail her now:
driving off into servitude as a
governess. Passing on her way a
glimpse of the sort of romance she
would surely never now know? –
smiling face upturned, fair head bent
to kiss the palm of a small white hand.
Absurd that, when later that moment
must be recalled, her heart should turn
over at the news that the lady
concerned loved the gentleman madly:
that the gentleman concerned was a
fortune-hunting rake.

Miss Bird – whom her pupil
christened, on account of those quiet
browns and greys 'Miss Dove'. But
who went to a ball, like Cinderella, in
a shimmering dress, and came to be
called by all her small world 'Miss
Radiant Dove'.

Whom romance didn't pass by, after
all.

ANNABEL JONES

The Radiant Dove

NEW YORK
ST. MARTIN'S PRESS

To Cobweb

Miss Audrey Rees-Webbe, with my love.

Chapter I

She had not named a time and there was no conveyance to meet her at the station, as she stepped down on to the platform, brushing the specks of ash and grit from her grey stuff travelling dress. A porter collected her basket-case and from the guard's van hauled out the big, domed black trunk. With much blowing of whistles and in a shower of sparks, the train gathered strength after its brief respite and chuffed on its way. 'Anyone to meet you, Miss?' 1823509

'No, I should like a hackney cab, if you please. But first —if I could arrange for my luggage to remain here a little while—?'

'You leave that to me, Miss, I'll deal with it. You'll be a new governess, then, for the Dower House?'

'I have applied for the post,' said Jane, a trifle stiffly.

'They always leaves their traps here, you see, in case they don't suit. And you wouldn't be the first had arrived prepared to move straight in—and been back within the hour and picked up her stuff and gone off home again. Though well rewarded, I dare say, for their trouble; her ladyship's always kind.' Though now and again, he added, laughing, hauling the trunk behind him as they walked—one of them might last as much as a month.

She longed to ask if the post were, then, so difficult; but would not demean herself. He waited for no questions, however, leading her out to the gravelled yard where a couple of old growlers stood plying for hire. 'She's a bit of a handful, the young one, I daresay; though sweet as honey in her pretty little ways. But where she won't tolerate, so they say, Mama far too easily gives in. To my mind, they choose them too old and ugly: that'll be Miss Ferris's doing, she pokes her nose into everything. Now, you're young and pretty, Miss, and has a pleasant way with you. The young lady will like that better, not a doubt of it.' He gave a sage nod of his head, handing her in, calling up the address to the coachman. 'Perhaps a shade *too* good looking, though you do dress so quiet, and keep yourself in bounds, I can see. But that's a fault on the right side.' And he gave her a nod again and a wink, slamming-to the door, closing her in in the darkness. 'Keep your pecker up, Miss!' he said. 'You'll do!'

Closed in the darkness: a bright world outside, the trees putting on their fresh new green, the meadows lush in the spring sunshine, distant hills rising up, bluebell blue. A man walking, whistling, his ugly old lurcher slinking at his heels, a smart barouche rattling by with a stout, prosperous gentleman handling the ribbons; a glimpse into a woodland romance—tall, straight back, fair head bent over a small gloved hand, palm held uppermost to receive a kiss; a farm cart rumbling with its heavy load behind two fine shire horses. A bright world outside: and she closed up in her temporary prison, en route for a prison of which the highest hope must be that it prove less temporary. Flight into servitude. Life had been dour and grim in these past seven years with her aged aunt, but it had not been servitude. 'You'll be a new governess, Miss?' A shade too pretty, he had thought her, though she did dress so quiet and 'kept herself in bounds'. Kept herself 'in bounds' to be kept in bonds and, devoid of other hope, must pray with all her heart for continuance in that bondage. And with some chance, it seemed, of her prayers being answered. The porter at the Robinstown railway station was confident that she 'would do'.

Anyone arriving at the front portals would be Madam or My Lady. Coming in a hired hack, Jane realised, one was simply a person. 'The Young Person, my lady,' announced white wig and red plush breeches, flinging open a door.

A slender figure, all in silks and laces, at the far end of the pretty, gilded room; seeming about to start up, settling back again. A second figure, rather tall, plainly but handsomely dressed, rising and coming forward. 'You will be the new governess, Miss Jane Bird?'

'The prospective governess, ma'am,' said Jane, bobbing a curtsey.

'Well, we will hope that this time—'

Hope! That word again! Had it come to this that after the long, dreary years with Aunt Philips one must set one's hopes so low?—immurement in a schoolroom, one's hair swept smooth and demure, one's looks, such as they might be, kept in check by drab dresses and no adornment: in a world between heaven and hell, between 'above stairs' and 'below stairs', a no-man's-land, belonging to neither; nobody's darling. 'Yes, indeed, Madam, I hope that I may suit.' She could hardly add that the station porter had felt sure of it.

'It's her ladyship who must answer that,' said the companion, leading her forward. She presented her formally: 'Miss Jane Bird, Cousin: the Dowager Lady Mellowes.'

The Dowager? Jane almost broke into a smile. Was this the dowager to whom reference had been made?— the letters had all been signed by Miss Hannah Ferris. This pretty, young, slim creature—a dowager? But yes; for she was the widow of the late Sir Randall Mellowes of the Great House of Robinsford; who, having no sons, had been succeeded by his younger brother. And she, if she had married young, need not be beyond the middle thirties—less, depending upon the age of the child whose governess Jane was to be. She said very sweetly: 'Miss

7

Bird—you've had a tiring journey from London. We sent to meet the earlier train but then were uncertain when you would come. You must have some tea and we can talk. Hannah—if you would ring?'

The companion cousin, with no very good grace pulled on a bell cord. She said as though Jane were not present: 'She's too young for the post: I warned you—she's young and she looks it.' And a great deal too pretty too, she did not overtly add.

'We wanted someone who would be a companion as well as an instructress. But we're asking a lot of you, Miss Bird,' said the little Dowager, shrugging with a comic little grimace. 'I'm afraid she *is* a *very* difficult child.'

'And Miss Bird has had no experience?' asked Cousin Hannah, returning to sit down next to Jane's chair, facing her ladyship's across the lovely high carved white marble mantelshelf. 'Companion to an elderly aunt, you said in your letter?'

'Yes. My aunt died some weeks ago. But as I also told you she had great nieces and nephews and I—well, perhaps I had best say that I supervised their education. And I understood,' said Jane, directly addressing Lady Mellowes, 'that some music and drawing and so on would be all the actual instruction required of me?'

'With embroidery, French conversation, reading in the classics,' said Miss Hannah. She asked in her rather lofty way: 'If you have lived with some aunt, how comes it that you are versed in these—sophisticated—talents? Music and drawing and what you refer to as "so on"?'

'My father was a man of means, Madam. But there were misfortunes and he died penniless. My mother endured a long illness and my aunt supported her. All I could do in return was to remain with her while she needed me: which was until her death. But I had already acquired my education and I used my spare time in trying to keep myself in practice.'

'And talking of practice,' said Lady Mellowes, 'a major

part of your task will be a constant practice in the French conversation my cousin mentions.' She fell into a little tinkle of laughter and said she supposed it was naughty of her, but practice in French conversation did always hold for her a sort of foolish hint of impropriety.

'I hope my conversation will be safe in that respect,' said Jane with an answering smile, 'in any language.'

'I don't know how improper Arabella's conversation may be, however,' said Lady Mellowes, ruefully. 'She really is a handful, you know. I do hope you're going to manage!'

Outside, the hackney cab still waited lest she must return to the station and make her weary way home. Hope rose in Jane's breast. If one must go out as governess, this pretty, elegant house with its pretty, elegant, smiling owner must be a great deal better than the vast majority that she might apply to. And one child who was a handful might be at least more entertaining than a dull resentful lump of girlhood or a wrangle of small, noisy boys. She said: 'Your ladyship seems to suggest—?'

'I suggest that we dismiss the cab,' said Lady Mellowes, smiling back at her.

The companion rose again to summon servants. 'Send the governess's cab away,' she said to the footman who answered.

'You'll see that the man's paid, James, please?' said Lady Mellowes, in her sweet way. To Jane she said: 'Your luggage?'

'I left it at the station, Madam. It seemed presumptuous,' said Jane, a little ruefully, 'to bring it to the house, as though I took employment for granted.'

'Well, it shall all be seen to. James will see to it for us, will you, James, please?' She said again: 'I hope you won't regret the decision, Miss Bird. Of course *I* think she's perfect; but she *is* very wilful.'

Jane thought back to the graceless horde of her aunt's young relatives. 'I'm not unused to controlling wilful young people. Some quite difficult girls; and even some difficult boys.'

'Ah, that's it: it's the boys that are the trouble,' said her ladyship.

'The boys?' said Jane, startled.

'Well ... To dowager old ladies like me—' began Lady Mellowes, with that laughing look of hers. But she broke off. 'Here she is now!' And there was a scutter of hooves on the gravel of the sweep outside the tall windows, a scudding of leather-shod feet across the black and white marble of the tiled hall. The door burst open and a voice cried: 'I saw the cab departing. Good!—she didn't suit, either? You've sent her away?'

'On the contrary—here she is!' said Lady Mellowes; and to Jane she said: 'My daughter....'

Tall hat swinging in a gloved hand, velvet riding habit fitting tight to a slender figure—auburn hair all tendrils and tumbling, blue eyes laughing, sweet face alight with triumph—and seventeen years of age at the very least. Miss Arabella Mellowes: whom all the world called Adorabella.

Jane's 'pupil'.

She stopped short in the doorway. The triumphant laughter died. She cried: '*You? You're* the new governess?'

'What a curious tone!' said Cousin Hannah from her seat in the corner. 'You sound as though you'd seen Miss Bird before.'

The blue eyes were a very dark, dark blue; the blue of deep water, not of clear skies—strangely lovely against the pale auburn hair. Now they stared straight into Jane's. 'Of course I've never seen her before!' And she challenged: 'Have I? You've never seen *me*—have you?'

Blue eyes, fair skin, pink-flushed, pointed face like a kitten's—looking almost fiercely into an oval face, pale-skinned, without colour, eyes hazel, hair almost hazel coloured also, drawn back neat and smooth from a wide, calm forehead. Calm only outwardly, however. Am I to start my life here with a lie? thought Jane—knowing too well that unless she did so she must find herself from the first moment of her employment with an enemy to deal with rather than a friend. She said: 'You may not have seen *me*. It's true that I have seen you.' She turned her eyes to Lady Mellowes. 'I passed Miss Mellowes out riding, as I drove here in my cab,' she said.

Something changed in the blue eyes. 'If you are to be my governess,' said her pupil abruptly, 'you had better come with me and let me show you your rooms.'

Cousin Hannah got quickly to her feet. 'I can do that, Arabella.'

Jane stood uncertainly. 'Oh, she only wants to question you,' said the girl angrily. 'Was I alone on my ride? Who was with me? Was it a young man, tall and fair? Was he riding too close to me? Whereabouts did we ride?' She looked directly into Jane's eyes again, but she spoke to Hannah. 'I would hardly ride alone. Of course I'd have a groom with me.'

'Miss Mellowes was accompanied,' said Jane. 'But I could hardly say by whom. Or indeed where; I came here in something of a dream—I didn't mark the countryside and indeed only looked vaguely at a pretty young lady with a very pretty chestnut horse.' She summoned up a smile, though she felt that she trod deep water, looking back into the blue eyes. 'I know a little of horses; I hope we'll ride together?'

'Well, you show her round, Cousin, if that's what you wish,' said Arabella, changing her mind as abruptly as she had formerly made it up. She came across the room and perched on the high fender beside her mother. 'How are you, my little Mama? Bored and lonely as usual?'

'I have had Cousin Hannah with me,' said Lady Mellowes.

'That's what I said—bored and lonely as usual,' said Adorabella.

It was a long room; very pretty, with its high painted ceiling, flowered carpet and delicate spindle-legged furniture, mahogany and walnut, brocade and gilt. Jane followed Hannah to the door and up the broad, curving staircase, two flights to the upper rooms. 'Insolent chit!' said Hannah, as the door closed behind her. 'Her mother allows her too much liberty—in speech as in everything else.'

'I think Lady Mellowes was chiding her,' said Jane. She asked: 'Excuse me, but I don't think I heard your name—?'

'Because it was not told you,' said Hannah. 'In this house, I am not in a position to be introduced.'

'I'm sure it was just that Lady Mellowes overlooked the matter.'

'Exactly. Would she overlook it, if we were two ladies of quality? Except that as it happens,' said the companion, with an air of haughtiness, 'I *am* a lady of quality. You appreciate that I am a cousin of the late Sir Randall Mellowes—and indeed of his nephew, Sir Dermot, up at the Great House, a generation removed.' They had stopped at the first landing and she gave a condescending nod and sketched a curtsey. 'My name is Ferris—Miss Hannah Ferris.'

She was—perhaps thirty-five? Middling tall, with a rather beautiful figure, full but graciously curved. Her complexion was dark, with an overtone of pallor, her hair very dark, straight and rather straggling despite its careful dressing; her eyes fine, only her nose rather long and pointed, spoiling what might have been something approaching real beauty. Indeed there was something altogether about her that was—spoiled. She is like a fine fruit, thought Jane, like a mellow pear which, however, when you cut it is dark at the core. In fact there was actually something almost pear-shaped about that curiously lovely figure; the rounded bosom, the swelling curve of the heavier hips. She said, in a voice of cold self-scorn: 'You will have taken it that I am the companion here?'

'I gathered that you were Lady Mellowes' cousin and companion.'

Hannah Ferris looked somewhat mollified. 'Well—that perhaps best describes it. I am of a cadet branch of the family, without wealth and therefore without consequence. When my parents died—at about the same time as Sir Randall died—and the widow, our Lady Mellowes, was obliged to move down from the Great House here to the Dower House—I came to assist her in her solitude and have remained ever since. That was almost ten years ago. Arabella was seven years of age.'

'Lady Mellowes seems very kind,' said Jane, toiling up the second flight, after her.

'Well, she's kind. She's impractical and—frivolous. And she spoils that child. I hope you will be a great deal more firm than she is.' She flung open a door and ushered Jane in. 'Though *I* consider you are a good deal too young,' said Miss Ferris.

The bedroom was charmingly furnished, frilled net curtains to the small, white-painted four-poster, flowered drapery and carpet, a small writing desk and an easy chair. 'The house does not allow for a separate sitting-room,' said Miss Ferris, 'but you can retire here when you are free to have some privacy; and for the rest, Dorabella's old schoolroom has been furnished as a sitting-room common to you both; she has, of course, her own boudoir.'

'It all seems very nice,' said Jane, looking round the room: wondering how many secret tears it might not yet see shed. She added: 'Did you call her by another name? I understood that she was Arabella?'

'That is her name; but they have this ridiculous affectation of calling her Adorabella, which we sometimes shorten. She was so christened by her cousin, Dominic, up at the Great House when first he came here, his father inheriting. He would be a great schoolboy then, but took a fancy to the child.' She shrugged. 'Which endures to the present.'

'And is returned?' asked Jane, thinking back to a recent scene: a casual hand on the bridle of a fine, spanking little chestnut, a flushed face raised, blue eyes a-sparkle; a tall figure stooping to kiss the inside of the wrist between a velvet cuff and light riding gauntlet.

'No, no, she thinks nothing of him,' said Miss Ferris, dismissing him. There were sounds on the stairs and she went to the door. 'Your trunk is arriving. I'll leave you to unpack your things. You will dine, at any rate tonight, with her ladyship and Miss Mellowes; and with me, of course.' She had suddenly become rather grand, issuing abrupt orders as to the disposal of the governess's luggage. Jane thought back to Lady Mellowes' gentle manner of asking: 'James will see to it all for us—will you, please, James?' Fortune was a strange thing; here was a woman who might have been pleasant and kind if life to her had been more pleasant and kind. Or was it she who had made it otherwise? Heaven forbid, at any rate, thought Jane, that she ever become my enemy! She felt that Miss Ferris would be anything but kind and pleasant then.

She finished the disposal of her small store of possessions, changed her stuff travelling dress for the new one bought for evenings—a governess's evenings. Fortunately, with her grey-brown eyes and the flawless almost colourless skin, pale browns and greys well became her. She had chosen a silk of almost the same shade as her hair, and yet with a silvery finish which she knew lit up her own quiet colouring with a sort of shimmer. But—for whom? she thought. Who would glance twice at the humble governess, permitted to sit 'for tonight, at any rate' with her ladyship and Miss Mellowes—and of course Miss Hannah Ferris? If there were guests, she supposed, a tray would be sent up to the converted schoolroom. It would not then be worth changing, even into the silvery brown. And at last ... Would not a day very soon come when Adorabella had succumbed to one or other of the adorers (she recalled that tall, slight figure, bent over the up-raised right hand) and she, Plain Jane, would be on her travels again?—would be sitting in another solitary bed-room, hardly likely to be so comfortable and pretty as this—a stopping stage en route for yet another strange bedroom, another house without interest in her except in as far as she could instruct and control ... She thought of Miss Ferris—well into her thirties, unmarried and grown bitter in her spinsterhood. What was there in this world for a woman but marriage?—a husband and chil-dren to love and to cherish; to be loved and cherished by. But Miss Ferris had been caught, one must suppose, between the fires of indigence at home followed by sub-jection abroad. A minor branch of a noble family; too conscious of position, perhaps, to stoop to where a humbler happiness might lie, too poor in fortune to move as an eligible girl among those who would seem eligible to her-self. 'I at least have no such complications,' thought Jane. 'A good-natured dustman would do very well for *me*.' But she knew that in fact a dustman would not do; and where, in her servitude, would she meet anyone that would? 'So perhaps I am as ill off as Miss Ferris,' she thought; 'only several steps down. *She* would not marry out of the aristocracy and none but a commoner will ask her; and I will not marry a dustman and who else will ever ask *me*?' And she thought again of that tall figure stooping over the little gloved hand; and wondered why she recalled the curve of a back, the shape of a bent head—in some odd way more clearly than she could conjure up the vision of the smiling, uplifted face.

A light tap at the door. Dressed now in white muslin with a sash to match exactly the deep blue of her eyes, Adorabella stood there. 'May I come in?'

Jane stood up. 'Yes. Please do.'

She came in and perched on the high window sill, framed in the background of sky and a tall cedar that made a dark pattern behind the little head, the auburn hair now combed and dressed, yet still in a rebellious escape of tendrilly curls. As Jane hesitated, she threw out a small white hand towards the chair. 'You don't have to stand upon ceremony with *me*. Please do sit down!' She looked her over with frank criticism. 'Why do all governesses dress in this colourless manner?' And she put her hand over her mouth and said, eyes laughing as her mother's eyes had laughed when she said that French conversation always sounded vaguely improper: 'You look like a bird indeed, Miss Bird. A little grey dove.' And then as a gleam of candlelight lit the silk to its delicate shimmer: 'But a radiant dove!'

'Governesses must behave like doves,' said Jane. 'I shall have to do something about the radiance.'

'Well, I've come with a little offering of birdseed,' said Dorabella. 'You got out of that very well—about my being out riding.'

Jane looked back at her steadily. 'I could hardly begin my post here with a downright lie—'

'So you began it with a downright fib! Now, come,' said Dorabella, laughing again, 'I was "out riding" it's true; but I wasn't out—riding.'

'Until I knew more of what was involved,' said Jane, 'I had to try to satisfy both parties.'

'And both *parts*—your conscience and your kindness.'

'I didn't want to make trouble for you—until I knew what the trouble was about. If you were doing something wrong—'

'It depends what is "wrong". I was doing what I am not permitted to do. And yet no one has specifically told me not to do it.'

'There is such a thing as obedience to the known wishes of those who—command us.'

'Ah, but that is it,' said Dorabella. 'Who commands

us? You yourself fumble for the word. And it is indeed a very big word.'

'Would you prefer—"advise us"?'

'I would prefer *not* to advise us"—or advise me, anyway. Why should I not meet Mr. Havering when I'm out—riding?'

'Well, you tell me,' suggested Jane, 'why should you not meet him?'

'Because they want me to marry Lord Brunel, that's why,' said Dorabella, bursting out with it. 'Because Lord Brunel's got all our land—well a great deal of it, of the Robinsford estate: he won it from my grandfather in a wager. And though they could buy it back, Lord Brunel won't give it to them. But if I were to marry him, then the estates—and our estate marches with his—would be brought together again. And so I am to be sacrificed: to this old creature, hobbling on a wooden leg—'

'A wooden leg?'

'Well, old and hobbling, a disconsolate widower. Was ever anything more ridiculous? For *me*! A man older than my own mother.'

Oh, dear, how awkward! thought Jane. Should I be receiving these confidences? But if they began within the first hour, she was likely to receive many more of them. 'Does Lord Brunel wish to marry? If he's still a sorrowing widower—?'

'Oh, well, as to sorrowing—he may have recovered from that by now. She's been ten years dead so I dare say he'll have got over it. He went abroad at that time and we've never seen him since. Still the fact remains that, grieving or not, he is to marry me. Not that he knows it yet, poor old thing: I daresay the idea will quite terrify him. But up at the Great House, they're adamant about it. My uncle thinks of nothing but The Estate and The Family; and he being now the head of it, of course Mama must not seem to disagree; and as for Cousin Hannah—'

'And Mr. Havering—stands in Lord Brunel's way, is that

it? Not that poor Lord Brunel seems to know yet that he even *has* a way.'

'Ah, well, Mr. Havering ... I'm afraid that with Mr. Havering, that's not the only objection.' Adorabella looked down into her lap and twiddled her thumbs: looked up, half scared, half naughtily laughing. 'Mr. Havering is—a Rake,' she said. 'And I love him madly.'

Absurd that a glimpse of a back view, a bent fair head, should make one's heart turn over with a tiny little somersault, at the news that Mr. Havering was an unacceptable rake: and that Miss Adorabella Mellowes loved him madly.

Chapter 2

A gong sounded its deep baying from the hall below and Dorabella jumped to her feet. 'Come, that's dinner!' And as she took Jane's hand and pulled her to the stairs, 'Not a word!' she said, conspiratorially smiling.

There was a guest after all. 'Your cousin Dominic called with a message from the House,' said Lady Mellowes, greeting her daughter with a rustle of pale green shot taffetas, 'and we persuaded him to stay.' To Jane she introduced him graciously. 'My nephew, Mr. Dominic Mellowes: Miss Bird, Dominic, who has come to be with us.'

'The new governess,' said Hannah Ferris, making sure he should understand it.

A dark young man, somewhat thickset, with curly brown hair and a quiet, rather conventionally handsome face and friendly brown eyes. He bowed. 'Miss Bird...'

'Miss Dove,' said Adorabella. 'I tell her that, in that silvery browny-grey dress, she looks like a little shining dove. A radiant dove,' she amended, looking over to Jane with her pretty face quizzically smiling. 'That was the phrase—Miss Radiant Dove!'

'I hope you will be happy in the dove-côte,' said Dominic Mellowes, bowing again; and he cast at Adorabella a look of tender indulgence. Isn't she sweet? that look said; isn't she comical?—isn't she entirely enchanting?

'A dove-côte indeed,' said Cousin Hannah, taking her

place at the table with an acid glance at Adorabella. 'And not too particular, I fear, as to what breed of bird flies into it.'

'You're referring to Mr. Richard Havering,' said Dorabella, coolly. She shrugged. 'At least he's not a doddering old widower whose lands you happen to covet.'

Miss Ferris bridled. 'I covet nothing for myself.'

'Don't you really? It would add to your consequence to be connected with a Robinsford Great House restored to all its former glories; and what else do you care about?' The blue eyes flashed contempt. 'What else *have* you to care about?'

Hannah Ferris looked outraged, Dominic unhappy; Jane herself felt acutely uncomfortable. Lady Mellowes protested. 'Dorabella, you are rude and unkind, my dear. What a horrid thing to say! Apologise, please, to your cousin.'

'Well, I'm sorry, Cousin Hannah. It was rude and unkind, I acknowledge. But *you* are rude and unkind to me —about Mr. Havering.'

'Mr. Havering is a man no young woman should associate with.'

'I do not "associate" with him. What do you mean by that word, please?'

'He is a rake and a libertine. It is known in the district.'

'A rake and a libertine—and lodging at present in the house of my uncle!'

'Your uncle cares only for his family researches and Mr. Havering assists him in the matter.'

'Mama receives him here.'

'Well, that isn't strictly true,' said Lady Mellowes, reluctantly. 'He is working on the investigation of the tapestry and that is in this house and can't be removed. I can hardly refuse your uncle; but you know, Adorabella, that we really can't approve unreservedly of Mr. Havering.'

'Just because you want me to marry this old dotard with his widower's weeds and wooden leg...'

The room was in curious contrast to that which Jane had first come to: the ceiling low and the windows leaded, the furniture in heavy oak with much carving. Dominic Mellowes, perhaps to disassociate himself from the argument now raging, explained it to the newcomer. 'This house has very old origins, much older than any at the Great House, up the hill. It has been much built on to, one wing, as you have seen, is not much more than contemporary. The architect has contrived it well, I think; the wings are at angles, never to be seen exactly at one time together. This part, of course, is early Tudor and the foundations go back possibly to Saxon days. And the tapestry...' He indicated it, a wide panel, running round four-fifths of the dining-room walls. 'Begun two centuries ago or more, retailing the history of the Mellowes family. My uncle is engaged in matching it with the records, searching out missing records to match up with *it*.' He smiled at her. 'A sort of family Bayeux,' he said.

'And Mr. Havering is helping him,' said Dorabella, intercepting the conversation. 'He is steeped in the study of the arts, the history of art, he's travelled half over the world—'

'And impoverished himself in doing so,' said Hannah Ferris tartly. 'Or in some other less creditable way, I daresay: but that is his story.'

The storm, never settled down, blew up again. 'You know nothing about it, Cousin Hannah, and nothing about *him*. Why is it your business?'

'Anything to do with the family is my business. Mr. Havering is reduced to taking a paid post with your uncle—'

Adorabella opened her mouth to make the obvious retort—but to Jane's great thankfulness had at least the grace to close it again, except to say more sweetly: 'He's of good family. What has money to do with it?'

'Only that he seeks to replenish his coffers by running after little heiresses,' said Hannah triumphantly.

The servants came and went, handing dishes, filling wine glasses; one must hope, unattending. But Jane thought she caught an exchange of glances between the elderly butler and his lady: she in her sweet, frank way almost appealing; he, respectfully affectionate, reassuring. Nobody in this household, she thought, would betray a mistress so kind and considerate, so gentle and sweet and gay. She herself sat silent and knew that she, at least, would not fail her in loyalty. 'I think,' said Lady Mellowes, imposing her will at last, 'that this unprofitable argument might now cease.'

'Yes,' said Adorabella, submitting at once. 'I apologise, Mama. And to you too, Miss Bird and Dominic. I have been very rude, at our own dinner table, to our guests.' But she glared back at Hannah with unrelenting resentment. 'We should keep our hostilities for exchange in private,' she said.

'If you would conduct yourself with propriety, there need be none.'

'Now, Cousin!' protested Lady Mellowes. 'Dorabella has apologised—very prettily too, I think. Let it end there. Only, my love,' she said to her daughter, 'I think we should not refer to Miss Bird as a guest. I hope you regard yourself as one of our household, Miss Bird?'

'I daresay she would rather not, after such an exhibition of the way we behave,' said Dorabella.

'You will sing her some of your ballads after dinner?' suggested Dominic. 'That will make up to her.' For anything, his loving look said; hear Adorabella sing and that will compensate you for anything!

And it was almost true. A delicious voice, thin, clear and fluting; and delicious little songs, lovey-dovey and nonsensical but spiced with a wit that robbed them of sentimentality. 'She composes them herself,' said Lady Mellowes, watching her fondly. 'Music and all. Don't you think that is charming?'

'I am stricken to recall, Madam, that I'm employed to "teach" Miss Mellowes music.'

'Ah, well, that means to compel Miss Mellowes, by whatever means you may, to perfect these accomplishments with some regular practice. And, dear Miss Bird,' said Lady Mellowes, 'I think that her Christian name will do very well. Or her pet name if you prefer.' She said a tiny bit anxiously: 'And I hope you do prefer?'

'I'm afraid she may be all you warned me of,' said Jane. 'But still I confess that she *is* "adorable".' And she took a sudden resolution. 'My lady—if I may ask you. I can't help but see already that there is at least some complication in Miss Mellowes'—in Adorabella's affairs of the heart. It may be difficult for me to steer a course between loyalty to my charge and to yourself.'

'Yes. It had not escaped me,' said Lady Mellowes with one of her smiling glances, 'that the complication has already arisen. I have an idea that you might not recognise the man accompanying my daughter on her ride today—but could not in fact have mistaken him for a groom?'

Not by any means *all* folly and frivolity, as Miss Ferris had slyly suggested. 'I had not yet had time, my lady, to adjust my priorities.'

'I thought you managed very cleverly. You threw at least one off the scent anyway; though I think perhaps that on reflection you were just simply not believed. My cousin is truly loyal to our interests,' said Lady Mellowes, 'though Dorabella is so naughty about it. But now, as to you...' She sat back in her chair, the pink striped brocade and gilded woodwork charmingly setting off the slim, still-young figure in the leaf green dress. 'I think I must simply put my faith in you. Do as you think best. If she will love you, she'll let you lead her. To betray her secrets, even for the best of reasons, will be to alienate her, and you'd be of no help at all.' But as she returned her hand to her lap and composed herself to listen again to the music, she did add, almost under her breath: 'But if we could see an end between her and this Mr. Havering—that, I confess, would be a blessing.'

'I wonder if she knows,' thought Jane, 'that he is permitted to kiss the inside of the wrist between the cuff and the gauntlet?'—that little, intimate kiss between two people in love. And in her heart again that foolish stab that said: I wish I did not know it myself.

The evening passed and the night and after a morning in which perhaps little was accomplished except the cementing of a comfortable relationship with her charge, Jane agreed to an afternoon's riding. 'Only I hope there's to be no assignation? That I couldn't agree to. Or, I think, keep to myself.'

Dorabella flared up immediately. 'Oh, well, if you're planning to peach on me when I tell you my secrets—'

'I simply say that I mustn't be party to them.'

'So that if we just met him accidentally—?'

'That sounds perilously near to a plan, Dorabella.'

'No, I promise you; I promise you there's no arrangement.'

They took a carefully chosen course nevertheless, Jane observed; and the auburn head, crowned with its high velvet hat and little feather, turned constantly this way and that as though in at least half expectancy. Apart from her anxiety, however, she found the ride delightful. Her horse was a strong bay, much heavier than the light, dancing chestnut which was Adorabella's delight and darling. 'Dominic gave him to me three years ago as a twenty-first birthday present. *His* twenty-first birthday,' she explained, seeing Jane's look of surprise. 'He said it would be the best gift he could receive—permission to give it to me. He persuaded my mother.' The chestnut was called Majority. 'I think it's an ugly name; but of course Dom had that day attained his majority.' She shrugged. 'It seems to please him; anything to keep him happy.'

'You were only a child then.'

'But he was already in love with me. Poor Dommie— he always has been and after all this time I suppose he'll not get over it.'

'You don't seem very grateful?' said Jane, ruefully smiling.

'Well—one gets used to things. And I do find that being loved becomes a trifle boring. In the beginning it's exciting; when first I came out, all the young men seemed to fall in love with me. I can't think why,' said Adorabella with a perfect innocence, 'because there were many girls prettier than I and a great deal more sophisticated, poor little country cousin that I then was. And I was— exhilarated—it was all such fun, flowers coming to the house morning, noon and night—that's the town house: now, of course, it belongs to my uncle but they opened it up for my debût. Though to be sure, they thought Mama allowed me to be presented far too young...'

'Perhaps they were a little in the right of it,' suggested Jane, smiling. 'Since at not yet eighteen you already find love and admiration so boring.'

'Oh, I only mean ... Well, I don't know: calf mooning ... Eyes gazing at you soulfully, hands beginning to tremble. You must agree with me?'

The horses had slowed down to an easy amble; along the narrow bridle path they rode close, side by side. 'I couldn't say,' admitted Jane. 'I must acknowledge to you that I have never experienced soulful gazing; nor seen hands trembling—not on my account anyway.'

Dorabella positively brought her horse to a standstill. 'You mean, you've never ..? But how old are you?'

'I have to admit to being nearly in the Lord Brunel class. I am twenty-four.'

'And never had a beau? But ... Well, you dress so mouselike and plain, and keep your hair so dull, but underneath that ... Why,' insisted Dorabella, palpably astonished to discover the quality in a governess, 'underneath that you really are *pretty*!'

'It's too sad then that none of the other sex appears ever to have observed it.'

'Oh, come Miss Bird! Not—not a Richard Havering, perhaps...' She put her little gloved hand to her mouth. 'Oh, that sounds rude—'

'On the contrary. From all I've heard of the gentleman, I should feel complimented.'

'That's very unkind; when I'm trying to be kind to *you*.'

'Well—we won't quarrel over it. The simple fact is that I have lived all these years and, pretty or not, no gentleman has ever even glanced my way.' And she thought of the grim, dark house and the grim dark old woman within; of the prison it had been through all her girlhood days, the charmlessness, the lack of all that for a young creature might make life worth living. 'I have been kept from the light, Dorabella,' she said. 'I am a plant that has grown in the dark and become etiolated without sun and air. I had to remain; at first so that my mother might be cared for; and then—well, I owed my aunt something; and perhaps the lack of light had already begun to tell, I had lost all the sap of my energy, I couldn't rouse myself to move elsewhere.'

'But to prefer to stay *there*!'

'What else should I have done? Only gone out as a servant.' But she recollected that in fact she had come out as a servant now; though, thank God! to a servitude of lightness and air. 'At any rate, I found no admirers for there were none to admire me. And now I can but hope to live vicariously in yours.' She made a little capital from the recital by adding that she wished Dorabella's might be such as she, in turn, could admire; though in other ways than love.

'Ah, and so we come back to poor Richard!' said Adorabella. She looked into Jane's face suspiciously. 'They've been preparing the ground; and for all your lack of sun and air, Miss Bird, I think they have found a rich soil.'

'You are so much like your mother!' said Jane. 'Beneath the outward appearance of easiness and what your cousin calls frivolity—you both have minds so clever and acute. You choose your simile, or carry on mine, very aptly. But no, I have not been instructed as you seem to suppose, no such seeds have been planted. I have eyes to see, however, and ears to hear; and where there are so many, it seems to me a pity—as it seems to your friends—that you should choose, as they consider, unfortunately.'

'Oh, well!' said Dorabella, dismissing it; though perhaps not with suspicions fully allayed. 'At any rate, it appears that for today at least your loyalties are not going to be too strongly tested.' They had passed through the narrow lane and now, in the lovely spring weather, jog-trotted in and out of patched sun and shade beneath the tall beech trees. 'This is the end of our path; he won't come today.'

'How do you mean—the end? The path goes on.'

'His path and mine. It ends at the great beech there. Beyond it, we are in sight of the Great House.'

'So you did have a plan? You've been deceiving me?'

'Certainly not,' said Dorabella indignantly. 'This is the shortest way between the two houses. So if he is coming to work on the tapestry—as he must often do—we may well meet: accidentally. There is nothing at all positive. I told you there was not.'

'All the same,' said Jane, rather stiffly, 'I think you have deceived me.'

Dorabella reined in her horse, pink with indignation. 'Deceived you? Am I deceiving you now, telling you that we meet—accidentally—when we can?' And indeed there was something about her, oddly frank and appealing. 'I think that's very unfair,' she said; and evidently believed it.

The Dower House stood in its own gardens but shared the

27

wide, walled parkland with the Great House. In the spring sunshine, it all looked very green and lovely. Deer grazed in a compact herd, raising their pretty heads to look at them as they rode by, mild-eyed yet tensed up, ready to scamper off if danger seemed to threaten. 'One day we'll ride through those woods,' said Dorabella, waving a gloved hand, her good-temper now apparently restored. 'They once belonged to us. They're Lord Brunel's now of course —if he really considers them so, being won in a wager— but we're quite free to go there. I've ridden that way all my life and all his men know me. It's true that he's back now from where ever he's been concealing his widowed griefs; but I daresay he won't come out, hop, hop, hop on his wooden leg, and charge us with trespass.'

Jane burst out laughing. 'Oh, Dorabella!—I'm sure he hasn't really a wooden leg?'

'No, no, I dare say not; all limbs present and correct as far as I'm aware. But you can't deny that at his age he can hardly be less than doddering.'

'Has no rumour reached you yet of how well he has worn in his absence? He's been away a long time. Really for ten years?'

'Oh, he's come back and forth, one understands, on the business of his estates—or our estates, as my Uncle Dermot would insist. But—he's been conscious, I daresay, of ill-feeling; at any rate, he's made no attempt at meeting us, on these brief visits. But now he returns for good and, with so close a neighbour, there must be some rapprochement. Meanwhile, he's an unknown quantity; or the number of his legs, at any rate's an unknown quantity. I'm condemned to wed him, sight unseen.'

'He may yet prove unexceptionable.'

'At his age? But what do they all care, anyway?—if he's bald and chumbling, toothless, palsied, stricken with the ague—as no doubt he is—one and all of those things— after all those years in foreign climes. And of course bent with sorrow, secret, misogynous, chilled to all unlove and bitterness ... What matter? He owns the land. That's it, my dear, he owns the land, and what else matters?—what is my happiness, my health, my very life as long as The Family gets back a few hundred acres of mud and trees that once belonged to our rude forefathers?' And she espied in the distance an aged farmhand and cried out that here was the monster approaching and they had better get home before he clutched and caught her in his skinny hands and carried her off to his castle. 'Besides,' she said, shaking the reins of the little chestnut, 'it's too late now. Richard evidently isn't coming.'

So—safe for one day at least. Jane took off her habit and asked for a warm bath to ward off possible stiffness—it was a long time since she had ridden and the bay was strong and a little hard to control. Bathed, dried, warmed in the sunshine flooding in through her bedroom window, she sat reading a little while and then, dressed in the silvery brown, went to look for her pupil. Dorabella was not in their sitting-room nor in her little frilly, foolish boudoir with its draped net curtains held up by winged pink and white cupids, its satin-upholstered chairs and scatter of Sèvres and ormolu. Nor was she in her bedroom. She was dressed, said her maid, tidying away riding habit and rest-gown, and had gone on downstairs. 'She's not with her ladyship, Miss, I know, for Bates has just gone to her.' Bates was Lady Mellowes' own maid. 'And Miss Ferris is dressing.' It was apparent from the slight toss of her head that Miss Ferris could dress herself and get on with it. 'So I've no idea, Miss.' But she gave Jane a small, sideways glance as if to say that she could perhaps tell a bit more; and didn't quite know if she should.

It was hard to know at first what was expected of one; whether or not to go on downstairs—Lady Mellowes had asked her to be with them again at dinner time—whether or not one should appear only when the gong went, modest and quiet in the brown dress, and slip into one's place, disappearing as soon as dinner was over, to the upstairs regions. Lady Mellowes was easy and kind, but one must not impose nor seem to take advantage. 'At any rate,' she thought with some bitterness, 'if I do the wrong thing Cousin Hannah is not likely to leave me long in ignorance. I'll go to the drawing-room,' she decided, 'and if Dorabella is there, perhaps I can glean through her what's the custom for governesses.' If she were not then one could just take a book and sit quietly in a window seat till others arrived; and when opportunity arose, ask Lady Mellowes outright. Still somewhat uncertain, she started down the stairs.

On the squared marble of the hall her evening slippers made little sound. She made her way across to the door of the drawing-room. From the dining-room to her right came a soft peal of laughter.

In the dining-room was the family tapestry, the 'Bayeux of Robinsford', as Dominic Mellowes had called it. And working on the research into the family tapestry these days, was Mr. Richard Havering.

'What must I do?' she thought. Could she, cowardly, continue to the drawing-room and pretend to know nothing? But she had said to Dorabella that there was such a thing as obedience to the known wishes of those who commanded; in this case who employed one. Must she go to the door then, and tap, and enter? What would they think of her?—what would *he* think of her?—walking in upon them like that—perhaps to surprise them in another kiss of the inside of an upturned hand. 'I can't,' she thought. 'I can't!' And yet ... But there was one way out: half courageous, half cowardly. If she were to let them know that she was there—could not the gentleman slip out of another door, could not the lady appear, all innocence, having been—having been re-arranging the flowers in a way that Mama would prefer them...? She gave herself no time for thought. She called out: 'Dorabella? Are you down here? Where are you?'

The door of the dining-room opened and Dorabella

came out and stood there, all smiles and happiness. 'Oh, Miss Bird,' she said, 'do come and meet Mr. Havering!'

Tall, she had known. Fair, she had known. But who could have guessed at the face that now smiled back at her?—the fine forehead, straight nose, wide mouth, sensitive and at this moment perhaps with a trace of humorous alarm in its smile; and all dominated by those bright, bright, brilliantly blue, piercing, laughing, dancing eyes…

Who could have guessed that her heart would take that now accustomed little somersault at the very thought of him?—would soar to the heavens and fall to her boots and resume its accustomed place with a fluttering of wild emotions as she stiffly curtsied to his low, just a tiny bit mocking, bow.

Who could have guessed that in the blue eyes there would have been—surely?—surely?—a small answering gleam.

Dorabella performed introductions. 'Miss Bird—Mr. Richard Havering. And, Richard, this is my Miss Bird—my dove, rather: in this shining silk dress I call her Miss Radiant Dove. Don't you think the name becomes her?'

She knew that a pink flush had risen up to stain the flawless pallor of her skin; rose from her curtsied greeting very slowly, keeping her head bent until it should die away. But Dorabella, her hand on Richard Havering's arm, stood laughing. 'Why Miss Bird, you're blushing! He is not so terrible as all that!' and to Havering she confided, 'You're right. Poor Miss Bird has been indoctrinated by the family to a belief in the total wickedness of all your ways.'

'It is true, alas!' he said with mock self-deprecation, '—that I am indeed a very dreadful fellow.'

Jane pulled herself together. 'Dreadful or not, Mr. Havering—Miss Mellowes should be in the drawing-room with her mother.'

'My mother is upstairs, still dressing,' said Dorabella,

'as you very well know. And so do I. I watched her maid go in before I stole down here.'

'You betray yourself with that word "stole", Dorabella. You shouldn't be here, alone with a gentleman.' Jane looked round the dining-room, at the tapestry banding the walls, the open books and papers on a side table. 'And Mr. Havering has work to do.'

'Let me show it to you,' said Havering, holding out his hand. 'It's quite fascinating, I assure you it is.' She did not take the proffered hand but she followed it, willy-nilly as it swept her round to face the wall near to the door. 'Here is where the earliest tapestry hangs. This part is over two hundred years old, two hundred and thirty-three to be exact. We can just discern, you see, the first Lord Mellowes arriving to claim his new property—this house, Miss Bird, this very house!—or this part of the house at least, where we stand now. It was here that the family first lived. Later the Great House was built, up there on the hill—in 1740 almost wholly destroyed by fire...'

'Look, over there in the corner, Miss Bird: that orange colour represents the flames.'

'The whole history of family and estate, you see, right up to the present day—or almost to the present: Lady Mellowes up at the Great House is working on the part relating to our times.' He led her to the following panel and this time she did not reject the touch of his hand at her elbow; though pretending in her absorption to be unaware of it. 'The work is done in panels, each panel to a generation. Some of the ladies have been lazy and contributed little; some unskilful and the work not very well done...'

'Poor Mama worked painstakingly at it till she left the Great House; but then thankfully handed it over to the new incumbent.'

'Is all the tapestry here? All succeeding generations? And why here?—why not the Great House?'

'It's all here,' said Havering. 'Or we believe so. Much was damaged, though we think none destroyed, in the fire. It was then that it was brought back to this house and re-installed where it had first been started. But it was not well done, panels have been put up out of their proper order, a great deal of it so badly affixed that it's impossible to remove it. Our work is, through the records, to restore the whole to its sequence, interpret events accordingly—and where records are missing, seek to discover those, in turn, through the interpretation of the tapestry.' His face was glowing, his eyes alight; the fine white hand pointed out here and there a detail. 'You see that by costume alone much may be deduced and dated. And see here, a small dog! Such a dog is mentioned in the diary of the third Lord Mellowes—'

'It was so sad, Miss Bird. His little son fell while playing with the dog, and died. So a cousin became heir and then we think that it was he who married this girl—here; and so brought the great beech forest into the family, the woods that now belong to Lord Brunel, the ones I showed you today ...'

'No, I have a new discovery there, Dorabella. It was the girl cousin that was heir, and so the question arose about the female line ...'

Jane noted the use of the pet name, and came suddenly to her senses. 'In any case, Adorabella, we must leave that branch of the family to its own troubles, and go to the drawing-room.' She said quite sharply: 'Come—if you please!' and bowed sketchily to Mr. Havering who, always with that faintly mocking smile, bowed back. 'Thank you, sir. It has been most interesting but we must go.' And she felt the blood mount up again to her cheeks and caught Dorabella's hand and turned away.

Turned away from the faintly teasing mockery of that bow which said, Yes, run, run away from the fox like a pretty little brown hen with your chick beneath your wing ... Turned away from the look in those bright blue forget-me-not eyes that said: but beware little hen—for the fox will get you yet!

In the drawing-room, Hannah Ferris was predictably awaiting them, irritably smoothing the folds of her dress of red brocade. Help she might not receive from the ladies' maids but she looked always handsomely turned out, affecting dark but splendid colours that set off her olive skin and the beautiful curves of her heavy figure; only, despite all her care, there was always that slightly straggly look of a stray strand of hair that would break away from the severe, smooth style and fall dark and lank until she pushed it back and tucked it away again. She said: 'Arabella—where have you been?'

Dorabella opened her mouth, no doubt to tell one of her all too easy oblique little fibs. Jane said as calmly as she could: 'Mr. Havering has been showing me the tapestry in the dining-room.'

'Mr. Havering?'

'He is working in there. No doubt he'll be gone before dinner is announced.'

'No doubt he will,' said Miss Ferris, grimly. 'But in the meantime—'

'Cousin Hannah, Mama allows Mr. Havering to come to the house. *Her* house,' added Dorabella, with not very delicate discrimination.

'Not to visit you, Miss, however. Miss Bird, I'm astonished at you. Where was your sense of propriety?'

'As long as I was with Miss Mellowes, there could be no impropriety.'

Hannah Ferris looked at her fixedly. She said at last: 'So that's it! You too!'

They stood grouped before the high white drawing-room marble fireplace under the sparkling light of the chandelier; crimson dress, pale, silvery brown, a frou-frou of muslin. 'I don't know what you can mean, Ma'am? What do you suggest?' But in the breast beneath the

34

brown bodice—Jane's heart beat wild and frightened as a little caged bird. 'I suggest,' said Miss Ferris, dark with anger, 'that you too have succumbed to the blandishments of this disgraceful young man.'

'He is *not* disgraceful,' cried Dorabella; in defence of her belovèd hardly observing the whole implication.

'It's hinted that ... Well, that is not for young girls to to hear. But the fact remains that he is a libertine and a gambler—cynically seeking to mend his fortunes by marriage to a rich young girl.'

'Then he'll hardly be bestowing his blandishments on me,' said Jane, seeking to draw the fire from her pupil, whose colour was now flying high, deep blue eyes ablaze. 'No one could call me rich; or even a very young girl.'

'You! Do you think he would be interested in you? But you're in charge of a promising victim; he makes love to the custodian so as to come to the goods he covets.' **1823509**

And alas!—how all too likely that was to be true. Whether cynically or not—and her idiotic heart protested against that—would it not be natural to exert a little of that easy charm so as to win over his lady's duenna to his side? She said, almost sullenly: 'Mr. Havering showed me the tapestry: that is all.'

'And so your colour mounts up at very mention of his name. You too are caught in this net of infatuation for a despicable rogue...'

And the door opened and Lady Mellowes came in; and with her, Richard Havering.

Mr. Havering bowed to the young ladies, bowed low to Miss Ferris, standing outraged in her dark red dress, with the one stray strand falling at the side of her face, flicked back, falling forward again. Lady Mellowes said: 'I found Mr. Havering passing through the hall on his way home from his studies in the dining-room.' She cast towards her cousin one of her half-humorous, half-guilty glances.

'He's been telling me of his latest discovery in the tapestry. It is so fascinating...'

'About the child that tripped over the dog, Mama?'

'Such a funny, prancing little dog! Have you never observed it, Cousin? In the right hand corner as you enter the dining-room.'

'I take no interest in the tapestry,' said Hannah, grimly. 'Nor in those who work on it.'

'There you're wrong on two counts,' said Dorabella, bursting out with it. 'The tapestry represents our family history and you think of nothing else. And "those who work on it" represent a way of life—freedom and lightness and gaiety, which you know nothing about and never could know and therefore pretend to despise, though at heart you envy it!'

They stood in stricken silence. Hannah Ferris and Lady Mellowes both cried out, the one outraged, the other reproachful. Adorabella burst into a storm of tears. Jane said quietly to Richard Havering: 'Perhaps you had best take your leave?'

'Perhaps I had, indeed,' he said, whispering back: and it was a conspiracy. He stepped forward. 'Miss Ferris. Miss Mellowes defends her—friends—and so whole-heartedly that in the defending, she in her turn offends.' He said to the weeping girl: 'You spoke unkindly; but for my part in it, I thank *you* for your defence and to Miss Ferris offer my apologies.' He added very sweetly: 'I know that when you are recovered, you will offer her yours,' and bowed to Lady Mellows and made a half circular movement so that his bow included the rest; and was gone. 'And if at least a little of each of four hearts does not go with him,' thought Jane, 'they must be hearts of stone.' (That little conspiratorial aside, that half appeal for help in a tricky situation! But she recalled the cold tones: 'He makes love to the custodian of the goods he covets,' and the small glow died within her.) She said: 'Come, Dorabella, come up to your room and bathe your face and compose your-

self before dinner!' and turned her glance towards Lady
Mellowes, asking permission to withdraw.

'I should never have brought him in,' said Lady
Mellowes. 'But I can't help saying it, Hannah: he is a very
—compelling—young man.'

'You are as bad as the rest of them,' said Miss Ferris,
and angrily thrust back the lock of falling hair, her eyes
resting hard and dark on Adorabella.

Chapter 3

A visit was proposed and Miss Bird must accompany the
ladies and call upon Lady Mellowes, up at the Great House.
The Dowager drove the short way there with Miss Hannah
in her pretty barouche. Dorabella and her governess rode
side by side behind the carriage. 'Miss Bird! Do you think
he will be there?'

Jane made no pretence of not knowing who was referred to. 'My dear, how can I know? But surely your aunt
and uncle don't encourage what your Mama objects to?'

'My uncle cares nothing about any of it; he's interested
only in the family archives and the tapestry history—
they were his hobby, and are become his passion since
Richard fired him with his own enthusiasm.'

'You refer to Mr. Havering, Dorabella.'

'He's Richard to me. Don't you think it's wonderful,
Miss Bird, that he can so immerse himself in the narrow
history of the Mellowes family when all the world is open
to him?'

Miss Bird did not suggest, even to herself, that Mr.
Havering might be interested in the Mellowes as his own
future family; let alone that so much expression of enthusiasm could arise from the necessity to continue in
this rich and comfortable refuge from his own penury:
clinging to it the more since it introduced him to a society
where he might meet and marry a fortune. Had indeed
already done so in the person of Miss Arabella Mellowes.

But Dorabella, though an heiress, had a mother still quite young and in most excellent health, and as Cousin Hannah did not hesitate to point out, there were many other strings to the gentleman's bow. Mr. Havering, it certainly did seem, was light of heart.

Dorabella refused to believe in serious rivals; and anyway, for the moment, as they trotted side by side along the forest ride to the house, had discovered a new amusement. 'Miss Bird!—I have suddenly thought of it. I have found you a husband.'

Jane, kept busy in controlling the strong little bay horse, could only say feebly: 'Good heavens!'

'The very man! Not rich, of course, and not—not of the aristocracy, certainly. But you would not look for that,' said Dorabella innocently. 'And between the two families, you might manage very well. Mama is already so fond of you, and the Great House will never dispense with Callie. You may always find an apartment there and the necessaries of life; and if you should have children—'

'My dear Dorabella! Who and what in the world—? Hey, Aldebaran, calm down, calm down!'

But the bay pulled hard on the bit, curvetting and stamping. 'We shall have to find you a quieter mount from my uncle's stables.'

'No, no, I can manage him. He's the lesser of my two handfuls. What is this nonsense you're up to now, Adorabella?'

'Why, Callie is my cousin Dominic's old tutor—but not *old*, you understand, or not very old: only in the sense of being discarded. Not that the Great House ever have discarded him; what he does to make himself useful there, no one in fact has quite discovered, but he and they alike all believe him indispensable. He's a dear, kind man— you'll see! Vincent Carrell his name is, but all the world calls him Callie as Dominic did when he was a little boy. He's everybody's friend, dear Callie, and so very understanding. And such great dark eyes, Miss Bird, you'll fall in love immediately. Now please do!' begged Dorabella, trotting her chestnut, moving smooth and docile, beside the prancing bay. 'I shall really be quite disappointed if you don't.' But her thoughts drifted away again. 'I wonder, will Richard be there?'

He was there; and so was the dark eyed Callie; and so were Sir Dermot and Lady Mellowes—and so was Miss Aurora Baines.

Miss Baines was the daughter of a gentleman as nearly 'in trade' as made no difference; but accepted in the county by reason of impeccable behaviour on the part of all his family and a refreshing absence of pretence. He was moreover of enormous wealth. Mr. Baines on this occasion was not present; but Mrs. Baines was there, enjoying a light repast of fruit and sweetmeats, and Miss Baines was there. And Mr. Havering was also there.

It was Cousin Hannah who first observed the crest on the Baines carriage door—Papa Baines made an open joke of the enormous trouble he had been to, to obtain recognition of it by the College of Heralds. 'How can our cousins admit such persons? Really, between riff-raff and plutocracy, the Great House is become a paradise for undesirables.'

'For my part,' said Dorabella, dismounting, handing over the chestnut to a groom, 'where the riff-raff reside, is paradise enough for me.'

'The riff-raff appears to be in very close attendance upon the plutocracy, however,' said Miss Ferris, glancing in at the tall french windows as they went up the great steps to the front entrance.

He rose to his feet as they entered, looking, Jane had to confess to herself, in considerable confusion. At the other side of the circle, a man also jumped up and stood respectfully bowing: a short, dark, stocky man, dark eyed, as Dorabella had said, with a sallow, round face and a fringe of black beard. Dominic also rose eagerly, his father more leisurely. Lady Mellowes put down needle and canvas and held out a ringed hand. 'Forgive me, my dear Rose-abelle; you know it's such a struggle for me to rise.'

Rose-abelle: a pretty name, thought Jane, for a pretty person. She had not known that the little Dowager bore it. She found herself presented to Lady Mellowes, curtsied, stood humbly aside as became a governess. 'Dorabella,' she hissed sharply to her pupil, keeping her voice very low. 'Your respects to your aunt!'

Dorabella was standing gazing with all her eyes at the plain, round face of the heiress: at the look of a wrong-doer caught out, on the face of her own lover. She collected her wits sufficiently to step forward and silently dip a curtsey to her elders; stepped back, fell into an urgent whispering. 'How *can* he? She's as ugly as—as the devil.' And over Jane's shocked repudiation of so unlady-like an epithet, she muttered wretchedly: 'Can it be really because she's so rich?'

Lady Mellowes was an old woman, more than half again as old as the lady of the manor whom she had succeeded; crippled by a rheumatism in the spine and hip, but with hands still strong and clever to dip the needle in and out through the great canvas, working in gros point the major scenes in the history of the family's past generation. 'Oh how wonderful you are!' said her sister-in-law, sitting down beside her. 'How I toiled!—and if I completed two square inches that was all I did in all my time as—well, while I was here.'

'And I've been half my time picking out your great stitches. You're a gypsy at heart, my dear Rose-abelle; fate should never have arranged for you to become a great lady.'

'A gypsy would not even have attempted the embroidery.'

'A gypsy would have had better things to do, binding up her offerings of stolen lavender and caring for her baker's dozen of children.' She cast an eagle eye towards where Jane stood with the stricken Dorabella. 'And bringing them up a deal better than you've brought up your one. You know that Brunel is arrived home?'

'You won't have much success in your plans for Lord Brunel, while you keep such counter-attractions here at the Great House.'

'Sir Dermot won't let him go: doting fool that he is! The young man is invaluable to him.' The keen eyes turned to where Richard Havering still stood beside the well-turned figure of Aurora Baines. 'At least there are counter-attractions as you call them, in another direction.'

A little apart Baines, mama, made civil conversation with that haughty spinster cousin of her ladyship's who, after all, was but a paid companion and yet gave herself such family airs. Dominic stood hesitant, not knowing whether or not his belovèd would welcome his approach to her. Richard Havering made up his mind. He bowed to the assembled company. 'If I may be excused? I should be working on the tapestry...'

But Miss Aurora, with eager insistence, put out a not very white hand and caught at his arm. 'Oh, I should like above all things to see it! If Lady Mellowes could possibly permit it—? I have heard so much of it, Ma'am, from Mr. Havering.'

'Has she indeed?' muttered Dorabella, resentfully, into Jane's ear.

'Yes, yes, we will all go down and see it,' said Sir Dermot in his hoarse, scraping voice. 'Lady Mellowes will give us permission, will you not, Rose-abelle? Mrs. Baines? —you will find it of the very greatest interest; the whole history of the family...' If he reflected that the family tapestry of the Baines would hardly cover a panel, he showed no sign of it. 'Come, boy, you can explain it to the ladies. And Dominic—?'

'I wished to ask Dominic to show me the stables,' said Dorabella. She spoke very coolly now and did not look at Richard. 'I'm anxious about the horse Miss Bird is riding; he pulls too strong. You might have something quieter, Uncle?'

'Help yourself, help yourself,' said Sir Dermot, uncaring. 'There's the grey mare, Honeycomb, too fat for any other work; just fit for a lady. I don't know why she wasn't offered in the first place.' To his ladies he confided, his harsh voice uncontrolled, carrying to the four as they obediently departed: 'That will separate the parties. Let Havering come with the heiress and leave Arabella free to her own devices. Or to his lordship Brunel's,' he added in what he evidently supposed to be an undertone.

Jane stood back to allow Dorabella to go forward with her cousin. Governess and ex-tutor followed in their humbler line of precedence. 'Poor child!' said Callie at once, looking pitifully after the younger pair as they walked obediently off through the long string of reception rooms and ante-rooms, out through a side door and towards the stables. 'Poor children!'

'Why do you say that?' said Jane; a little astonished at his easy frankness.

'Both so much in love; and both with the wrong people.'

'Mr. Dominic Mellowes makes no secret of his feelings for his cousin.'

'Nor she of her feelings for another; though she should know better.'

'In loving? Or in showing that she does so?'

'In both. A young lady of breeding should have herself under better control; as must lesser mortals,' he added on an odd little note of ruefulness. 'And as for the gentleman —well, I sadly fear that he really is not worthy.'

She felt that so intimate a conversation, relating as it did to the private affairs of their employers, was perhaps not wise—and upon so very short an acquaintance; but in seeking for words to cover over her own stab of pain at that word 'unworthy', found herself still continuing it. 'You too are for the match with his doddering lordship?'

He laughed, looking at her appreciatively with those

large, dark eyes and she thought to herself that yes, he was a nice man, as Dorabella had said: understanding and kind, with something so frank about him as to be almost naïve. 'Doddering! You've been talking to the Wicked One herself,' he said.

'About the Wicked One *him*self: about Lucifer with a forked tail and hooves—or one hoof, rather; she goes so far as to endow him with a wooden leg.'

He laughed again, outright. 'Well, it's true that we know nothing of him. Nothing of him personally that is.'

'Only that he owns what she calls some mud and trees; and that she is to be bartered in exchange for them.'

He made a little rueful grimace. 'It's only in recent history that young ladies had any choice at all. But no one would really marry off Adorabella without her consent to it.'

'*Her* consent? To a man older than her own mother?'

'That's an accustomed refrain,' he said. 'But older than Lady Mellowes leaves him still but in young middle age. And does but repeat her mother's own case. Sir Robert Mellowes had been widowed and was more than twice her age when she married him.'

'And so became, hardly out of her twenties, a dowager, dispossessed of her home and high position.'

'Dorabella must take care to provide herself with a son against such eventuality. She may then reign at Brunel Hall—as regent at least—until her son marries. And the Dower House there is delightful.'

They had come to the stables. Dorabella was putting a good face on things, very clinging and possessive with her cousin as though to show to the absent Richard how well she could do without him. Jane protested her entire ability to manage Aldebaran despite all this sudden anxiety on her behalf, but the stout little grey was brought out nevertheless and paraded. Dominic with a bound got himself astride and rode her bare-backed around the yard with no more than the halter. 'See how biddable she is,

Miss Bird! You'll find her tame as a tortoise.'

'And about as speedy,' said Jane, protesting. But she recollected her position; in this company it was too easy to forget that she was not just one of themselves. 'It's as you think best; I have no complaint whatsoever, myself, of my beautiful Aldebaran.' She said to Dominic, apologetically: 'Of *your* beautiful Aldebaran.'

'He shall be yours as long as you want him,' said Dominic, 'with all my heart. It was my cousin who was concerned for you.' He looked at her young, strong, slim figure, compact in the well-cut riding habit. 'I can see that you're well used to riding.'

'You see that my riding-habit is well used to being worn,' said Jane, smiling. 'It's the one I had when I was almost a child; before my father died. It hasn't had much use since, but it had plenty then.' She had been deeply relieved, on finding that she was expected to ride with her new pupil, to discover that it still so well fitted her.

He made her a little bow. 'If I may be allowed to say so—it becomes you immensely.'

'More than her mouse-brown dresses?' suggested Dorabella. 'She does no justice to herself, I tell her.'

'I do justice to my position,' said Jane, coolly. 'A fine thing if the governess were to appear in—fine things,' she ended, laughing.

'Nevertheless, I should sometime like to see it,' said Dominic.

'And I,' said Callie. 'The radiant dove, Adorabella calls her. I should like to see her in a gown the colour of a different kind of dove: a gown shimmering like the plumage of a pigeon, pale iridescent greens and blues. Close hugged to the figure and then all soft movement as though the glowing feathers were ruffled by a little breeze...' He too sketched a bow, half apologetic. 'You must forgive me. I fancy myself as something of an artist. I see you in such a dress: I should like to paint you in it.'

'Yes, Callie, you must paint her.' Dominic threw a leg

across the stout pony's neck and slid down, facing them. 'I saw just such a taffetas at the dress-maker's, last time I went on some errand for my mother there. With just a short length of it, you may concoct the whole dress in your mind: it's in your mind already.' He patted Honeycomb's round rump and sent her off back to her stable. 'Adorabella —Callie must paint our Miss Shimmering Dove?'

'Yes, indeed; and make copies for all her admirers,' said Dorabella, almost sharply; and hooked her arm into his and started off back to the house with him.

'Miss Bird, beware!' said the tutor, offering his arm, turning to follow them. 'You are in danger of making Adorabella jealous.'

'Mr. Mellowes makes himself agreeable to the custodian of the goods he covets,' quoted Jane, a trifle bitterly; and could not forebear to add, 'And not the only one to do so. I mean,' she said quickly, 'that that is the way of the world. I make no special reference.'

He turned to look keenly into her face. 'Has life already taught you so hard a lesson?'

'I'm not a child,' she said.

'But have not long been a "custodian".'

'For one in my position,' she said, shortly, 'there are ready instructors.'

He slowed down their walk to a dawdle. 'We are in an equivocal position, Miss Bird, you and I.'

'And it behoves us to remain exactly in that position.'

'In this family, you will find that it doesn't too much restrict us.'

'For my part,' she said, bitterly again, 'I have found that not universally so.'

He smiled, a little ruefully. 'I think perhaps I know what you mean. But ... When we first come to— dependence—Miss Bird, we're apt to look inwards and see none but our own humiliations. You'll learn, however, that you're only one of a huge company, of the vast majority, subduing their proud hearts to the situation this world has placed them in. You say that we should keep ourselves to that situation. Yes, you're right: to try to struggle up from it is to court disaster, and that I have learned to my very bitter cost...'

'You? You seem almost on an equality here?'

'With some,' he said, briefly. But he smiled again, and lightly pressed the hand tucked into his arm. 'Come, Miss Bird—you and I are fortunate; our yoke is a very light and kindly yoke. Let's be thankful for that; we have only to bend our necks just a very little and it won't chafe us. And you and I, I hope, may be equal, and therefore easy, friends?'

'In that indeed I shall be fortunate,' she said; and smiled back at him gratefully and with a heart more at ease, went on with him to the house.

The party had arrived back from the Dower House and were in fine fettle; the tapestry had proved of absorbing interest and Mr. Havering so clear in his explanations ... Miss Aurora made little secret of her regard for him as her property, at least for the moment. 'Such fun we had, it was delightful! We all crowded into the carriage, not worth putting up the horses in your barouche for so short a trip; and finely packed in we were, I had almost to perch myself on Mr. Havering's knee!'

'Mr. Havering would have been too happy,' said Richard, gallantly.

'And doubtless would have managed with you perfectly,' said Dorabella, smoothly. 'One hears that he is not unaccustomed.'

'We have been concocting a plan,' said Callie, hurriedly intervening to prevent any further outburst of pique, disclosing ever more overtly her jealous preference. 'I am to paint Miss Bird, she is to sit to me—'

Jane hurriedly disclaimed. 'Indeed, no such arrangement was made or thought of.'

'It may not have been made but it's being thought of,

47

and at this very moment. I see her as Miss Mellowes has named her,' he said in his eager way to the assembled company, 'in a dove-coloured dress, not the soft grey dove but its sister, all iridescent plumage of greens and blues. Dominic tells me there's such a stuff to be had at the dress-maker's in the town. I shall buy a short length, just enough to give me the drapery...'

'You must wear your hair just as it is, Miss Bird,' said Aurora. 'Very smooth and shining, like the dove's sleek head; and wear flowers in it, pale pink rather waxy flowers, like the dove's bill.' She stood smiling with a simple generosity, the plain round brown face looking into the pure oval and the long-lashed, hazel eyes. 'It will be a lovely picture,' she said. 'You will look lovely.'

Mrs. Baines was embarked upon farewells. 'Come, my love, the horses are put up so we will not unsettle James Coachman again, but now take our leave.' As Richard Havering bent over Miss Aurora's hand, however, she murmured, under cover of leave-taking: 'Who *is* the young gentleman?'

'A cadet of the Haverings of Norfolk,' said old Lady Mellowes, promptly. 'Full of charm. And so clever. Sir Dermot quite dotes on him.'

'And eligible? One has to be ... Especially in her case, if you will not misunderstand me, one has to be so care-ful.'

'A younger son; and I believe has no money.'

Mrs. Baines was too recently well-bred to reply that that need be no hindrance. 'You would have no objection to my including him in an invitation to our next ball—which your family, of course, will shortly be receiving, if they will honour us.'

'No objection in the world,' said old Lady Mellowes, mellifluously; and her look after the departing lady said, to Jane's observing eye: 'Good—that may well have got rid of *him*!'

Adorabella stood chattering to Dominic. His handsome

young face looked back into hers with a mixture of delight and sadness; irresistible she might be and was, but he was far too intelligent not to understand that she was using him in a game against Richard Havering. She walked on with him to where the barouche now awaited them, a groom at the horses' heads, another man standing holding the bay and the chestnut as they shifted and scuffed the gravel with impatient hooves. Vincent Carrell squired the Dowager, Rose-abelle, down the sweep of marble steps. Jane making her quiet farewells to her hostess, found herself held back. 'Well, Miss Bird—are you happy in your new employment?'

'Very happy, my lady, I thank you; the more so as it's my first and I didn't know what to expect—dared not look for such kindness.'

'Ah!' The faded eyes looked keenly back into hers. 'Well—poor child! We can't control the paths of your life, but we shall all do our best, I know, to make them sunny and pleasant while they run through our country. And you, in turn, will accept our trust and closely guard our treasure?'

Your treasure is some mud and a few trees, thought Jane. *You* think it's a lovely young girl but the reality is different, you would all place landed possessions before her happiness. She was touched, nevertheless, by the kindness shown her, dismissing any thought that it had been only leading to a reminder of her duties. She looked down to where Dominic was helping Dorabella to mount, brushing aside the groom's proffered hand, holding his own for her little foot to step into. A skip and a jump and she was up, sitting with her velvet knee over the pommel, skirts trailing over the pony's flank, the reins gathered laxly in her gloved hand. All her face was alight with smiles, the auburn hair tossed this way and that, beneath the tall riding hat. To Richard Havering, walking back from the departing Baines carriage, she smiled with utmost sweetness and turned away immediately to continue conversation with her cousin. Havering bowed deeply in farewell and left them there, springing up the steps to the terrace. In a moment he appeared, framed in the tall french window.

If she expected him to be shame-faced, downcast, apologetic—Jane was disappointed. His face was alight with vivacity and interest. 'Oh, my lady—can you tell me where to find Sir Dermot? I believe I have discovered a secret sign, hidden in the tapestry!'

Chapter 4

So for some days Mr. Havering came no more to the Dower House, except once or twice to be closeted alone with Sir Dermot in the dining-room, seeing nothing of the family; and Adorabella rode no more along the bridle path towards the great beech tree. Nor was it Richard, Richard any more, in her idle chatter; she worked hard at her studies, but restlessly, her little face was pale and listless, the deep blue eyes shadowed, the very ringlets of her hair seemed to droop without their customary gloss. Her mother watched her unhappily, Cousin Hannah with a sort of cold triumph. Hannah was back and forth, visiting the Great House, Jane knew, arranging for a form of meeting with Lord Brunel. Sir Dermot had made a morning call in formal welcome of the return of his neighbour but was too cross and resentful to do more than report that he seemed a proud-spoken, ill-natured fellow as he ever had been, and that was all there was to him.

The pride might be only in possession, however; and the ill nature in not offering to return the wide acres acquired, in all honesty, since a wager was binding to any gentleman. At least there appeared to be no suggestion of an invalid chair.

Lady Mellowes proposed an excursion to the neighbouring town. 'We'll borrow your aunt's phaeton, if she has no use for it this afternoon, and go in style. I need to match some threads for her tapestry; she's so particular, Callie alone never gets them quite right for her, and she can't go herself. Will you not be amused to see this great new emporium, Dorabella?'

'Mama, I can scarcely breathe for excitement at the prospect.' But she went over and gave her mother a little, grateful kiss.

Lady Mellowes having sent off a message to the Great House, called Jane over to her. 'Miss Bird. I am in a tiny embarrassment; you're so kind that you'll forgive me if I seem to offend you in any way—but I think it best to consult you, yourself, about it.' She held out a large white card. 'The invitation to Aurora Baines' ball at The Towers. It includes your name.'

Jane lost colour a little. She said at once, however: 'They haven't understood, ma'am, that I am the governess. You all treat me so kindly that it may have been not apparent.'

'Oh, she must come!' said Dorabella. 'You must come, Miss Bird.'

'My dear, I think Miss Bird won't wish to accept, under a misapprehension.'

'No, certainly not,' said Jane. 'I couldn't bear it.'

'You must come! If you have no dress, you shall wear one of mine.'

Jane laughed: 'Squeeze myself into one of your fairy-doll costumes! The hooks and eyes wouldn't meet round me by three inches. In any event, of course I couldn't possibly go.'

'I can only say,' admitted Lady Mellowes, 'that I think you are right. You wouldn't want to go there under false pretences.'

'I have made no pretences, my lady,' said Jane, suddenly nettled; but she recalled the too easy familiarity with which she had conversed while they all discussed the grey pony in the yard at the Great House; and how she had then felt obliged to remind herself of her position.

She said more humbly: 'I beg your pardon, my lady. I know you made no such accusation.'

'I used an unhappy phrase, perhaps; forgive me!' But Jane thought that Lady Mellowes looked at her with a glance more appraising than heretofore. 'She has seen me as nothing but the governess,' she thought, 'simply out of habit. Now it comes to her that I am, though now in an inferior position, after all born a lady. A few weeks ago I might have accepted such an invitation without a qualm.' The older Lady Mellowes had seen more clearly; or perhaps looked more carefully. The Dowager cared nothing for anyone's situation; from the highest to the lowest, all were equally fit for her consideration. Lady Mellowes at the Great House looked deeper; she looked below the surface and saw, not only her own manner, but also the effect it must have according to the recipient.

The spring weather lasted, it was a perfect day to be driving out in the open phaeton, their ribbons fluttering in the faint stir of its movement, Dorabella's hair like a pale flame flickering, beneath the tilt of her foolish little flowered hat. Callie had been sent down with the phaeton, full of careful instructions about the matching of the threads and they had persuaded him to go on with them. He sat with Jane, backs to the horses, in the seat facing the Mellowes ladies and Miss Ferris. On either side, the fields and woods, fresh in the season's soft new green, passed like a painted landscape beneath a blue sky patched with fleecy, painted clouds. Callie chattered away in his comfortable fashion, never over-familiar and yet ever unaffectedly easy and at home. He was in fact a clever artist and invaluable to Lady Mellowes up at the Great House in the designs of the latest panel of the family history. 'You can't imagine our struggles to bring in the loss of the estates to Lord Brunel, without too much offending Sir Dermot's susceptibilities! And yet it must be shown. And Havering's no help, he and Sir Dermot are mewed up for ever in their den of dust, over this new discovery in the tapestry.' He brought in casually a name which, since the morning visit, had not been spoken at the Dower House.

'Tell us about the discovery,' begged Dorabella, as casually; not loath, perhaps, to hear that name spoken again.

'Some small black mark in the panel which represents the early eighteenth century. Up to now it's been supposed to be just the scorching of the fire in 1740. Now Havering has observed that the mark is in fact a tiny row of stitches, deliberately placed there.'

'What can that be taken to mean?'

'I have no idea,' said Callie, as the rattle of cobbles under their wheels signified their entry into the town. 'And neither have Lady Mellowes nor Dominic. And no chance to ask questions: those two are unapproachable, heads always together over their investigations; even their meals are sent in to the study. I think they have hardly emerged from it since you last saw them.'

'One at least has emerged from it now,' said Miss Ferris. She indicated the closing door, yellow-painted, of a small house cramped into a row of similar pretty little houses, giving straight on to the street. 'And by the look of it, only to go directly to a den of some other colour.'

Dorabella swung round, startled out of her self-absorption. 'Do you mean it was Richard?'

'Well, it was not your uncle,' said Miss Hannah, sourly.

Callie looked vaguely uncomfortable. 'Perhaps you were mistaken?—' but Dorabella persisted. 'What can he have been doing there? In such a place as that?'

'Come dearest, Mr. Havering's affairs are his own,' said Lady Mellowes, mildly reproving.

'I choose to make them mine also, Mama; and I say— what can he be doing there?'

'Then I must tell you, my dear, that you're behaving badly. Now come, we are arrived; put on a presentable face, if you please—the place seems crowded, you don't

54

want to advertise your personal feelings to the whole world, I take it?'

The matching of the threads was a long and exhaustive business. Cousin Hannah took charge of Dorabella and pioneered a way through the shop, pointing out the variety of goods and their excellent arrangement. 'Yes, Cousin. Yes, yes, I find it quite beautiful, Cousin,' said Dorabella, petulantly following.

Jane stood quietly in the background lest Lady Mellowes require her attendance. There Mrs. Baines came upon her. 'Why—is it not Miss Bird? We met at the Great House. Aurora—Miss Bird!'

Jane looked rather helplessly to where Lady Mellowes stood absorbed in colour and texture. She said at last, deliberately: 'I was there with my—waiting on my—my pupil and charge, Miss Arabella.'

'Your pupil? Why I had thought—'

'I am aware of that, ma'am. And perhaps, as this meeting has come about, I'd better speak out frankly. You have been so very kind as to include me in an invitation for your forthcoming ball. I knew at once that you had not recognised me as only the governess—'

'The governess? Well, no, indeed I had not; you are not at all my idea of a governess.'

'I was in riding habit, ma'am; in my mouse-brown walking-dress, you'd have had no such difficulty.' She smiled to show that she felt no resentment. 'I had arranged with Lady Mellowes simply to declare myself unable to accept, without troubling you with the reason.'

'And a very bad reason it is,' said Mrs. Baines, roundly. 'Why should you not come to the ball, if you *are* a governess? A very pretty young woman and, plain to see, a perfect lady. Pray ask Lady Mellowes to bring you with her party.'

'Indeed, Madam—'

'Miss Bird, we shall take no refusal—shall we, Mama?' said Aurora, standing by, her plain face lit up by the friendliness of her smile. 'We insist upon it.'

'I shall be out of my place. I don't say it in anything but the purest simplicity,' said Jane, flushing all the same, a little. 'But who will wish to find himself dancing, at a county ball, with a stranger who turns out to be his neighbour's governess?'

Mrs. Baines laughed her fat, friendly laugh. 'Oh, my dear, don't trouble yourself on that score! Do you think we invite none but the high aristocracy? We made our friends when our circumstances were more humble and we don't forget them. Those who won't meet them at our house, are welcome to remain away; and your stranger who feels himself demeaned in dancing with a governess, may stay away also.' She bowed very kindly and passed on, her great skirts whisking away the careful setting of a display of laces. 'Do come!' said Aurora. 'Mama means it. If you don't, we shall know it and send a messenger to fetch you.' But Jane thought that she looked her up and down a little scrutinisingly as she also swept on, following her stout mama.

'I shan't go,' thought Jane, however, watching their somewhat bustling departure. 'What should I wear?' The thought came into her mind that Lady Mellowes might, in her generous kindness, insist on repairing that lack, and she decided to make very little of the encounter. 'I met with Mrs. Baines and her daughter while I waited,' she would say, 'and told her that I must decline her invitation to the ball. She put up some sort of civil insistence, she was very kind; but of course it wouldn't be suitable and I prefer not to.' To seem to wish to go, to push herself forward, to hint for a present of suitable wear, made her blush with a sudden proud humiliation. 'I shall let them suppose that I don't dance,' she decided. 'That will clinch it.' (Oh, the dancing lessons of long ago, with Papa so much enraptured by her progress, Mama so happy in the beauty and grace of her darling! The gone, dead days of happiness long past! 'Still, how happy am I now,' she thought, 'in comparison with the years between.' And with Dorabella's complicity, it seemed, she might even yet find a husband—in Dominic's 'old tutor'!)

And she heard Callie's voice behind her. Lady Mellowes still bent, absorbed, over her purchases, but he had evidently spied an acquaintance and stepped aside. In the crush he apparently did not see her. He was saying: '... a small house in Capsicum Street. I saw him enter.'

'He keeps some sort of establishment there,' said the other voice. 'I think he does not want to be totally dependent on his present situation.'

She felt that she should move away, but was held prisoner by the crowd; might have made her presence known but now the stranger's voice continued. 'I have heard him say—lightly, a little in his cups—that he went there to visit a lady. Or kept a lady there; that was the way of it, I now remember.'

'Some relative,' said Callie, quickly. 'Some indigent relative or friend...'

'No, no, my good Callie, you can't get out of it that way! The lady is young and beautiful and—a foreigner. More and more comes back to me as I recollect the occasion.'

'Well—he has been abroad. There may be many explanations.'

'Choose one to suit yourself. The fact is, isn't it?—that you are not quite happy about him: for he has his hooks well fastened into your pretty Adorabella?'

'Miss Mellowes is acquainted with him, naturally,' said Callie, coldly. 'He lives in her uncle's house.'

'Well, come, my dear fellow, you needn't be so stiff about it! What woman that sees him remains simply "acquainted"? And why else your interest in Capsicum Street? Not but that I'm sorry for it. Miss Mellowes is a charmer and I'm sure deserves a great deal better. But they say he is out after the Baines girl now; the whole family quite dote upon him. Mama Baines should know of his—

acquaintance—with the Honourable Clarissa Townes—
as no doubt you do yourself? And of a recent brush with
that imperious Rutherford girl. Heiresses both! Not to
speak of—and certainly one should not speak of—the
beautiful Mrs. Edgar Worcester who lives in Mayfair:
without *Mr.* Edgar Worcester.'

'I have not the honour to know anything of Mrs. Edgar
Worcester.'

'There is nothing of honour *to* be known about Mrs.
Edgar Worcester,' said the gentleman laughing; and, the
mob parting a little, went his way.

Blue, blue eyes—forget-me-not-blue, unforgettable blue
looking down into her own with that small, that tiny
spark of an answering gleam! 'Young ladies may suffer
and sulk,' thought Jane, 'and be petted and coaxed back
to happiness, guarded from harm. But what is a governess?
A creature who may be permitted, I suppose, in obscurity
to break her heart; overtly may not even admit to a heart
to break.'

But here was one governess at least, with a heart to
break; and that heart at the mercy of a gentleman who
came from the charms of disreputable ladies in town, to
the pursuance of wealthy young ladies in the country—
and who kept, it would seem, a lady of his own in a small
house in Capsicum Street.

For even Callie had been unaware—had been obliged,
in his jealous care of the precious treasure of the Dower
House, to make enquiries—of that house in Capsicum
Street.

They overtook him, riding back to the Great House. He
saluted them gaily, followed the carriage at a trit-trot; was
there to help them alight as they came to their door. Lady
Mellowes said as she saw him turn in at the Dower House
gates: 'Now, Dorabella!—demean yourself correctly. Show
no pettish resentment. Simply behave as to any gentleman
of your acquaintance.' Her face had lost its customary easy

smilingness. 'I don't often admonish you but this time I am quite in earnest. Don't let yourself down!'

'And let the same apply to me,' thought Jane, preparing to follow the ladies, handed down by Callie. She saw how Dorabella obediently dipped her curtsey, with a stiff smile accepted his greeting. And now it was her turn. The blue eyes looked down into hers. 'Miss Bird.' A little pink, perhaps, had sprung up in her cheeks, brightening her eyes. He said, but he said it to the assembled company, lightly: 'The outing has done Miss Bird good. There are roses in her cheeks.'

Her colour heightened. Lady Mellowes said, keeping the atmosphere easy and without tension: 'In fact I often think of Miss Bird as a rose—a wild rose, as one sees them in the hedgerows; an eglantine.'

'A blush rose after all these compliments,' he said, still holding her hand, still looking down at her. But he seemed to recollect himself and rather hastily released her. 'Have the ladies enjoyed their visit to the new palace of haberdashery?'

'Oh, charmingly. We met all the world there. Mr. Broderick, squiring his sister,' said Adorabella, 'and Sir George Pringle and his brother, like lost lambs among all the ribbons and laces, having lost touch with their mother ewe. And Miss Bird met Mrs. Baines and Miss Aurora, who pressed her to come to their ball; but she will not, though Aurora insisted.'

'Miss Baines was very kind,' murmured Jane unhappily; Adorabella spoke the names of her admirers—and of his admirers also—with apparent indifference; but the point could hardly be lost upon her hearers.

'I think she *is* very kind,' said Richard Havering, coolly. 'I have met her again, recently, and though she openly lays no claim to beauty, she is clever and charming.'

'We thought you had been closeted night and day with my uncle?'

'It was while on an errand for him that I encountered

the family—just entering their gates. They so pressed me to stay for a moment that I couldn't refuse without ill manners. I called in for a moment.'

'We have been less fortunate at the Dower House,' said Adorabella. 'But of course we have been less pressing.' She smiled and bowed a dismissal. As she swept away after Lady Mellowes up the steps of the house, he said aside to Jane who stood, like a stricken rabbit, powerless to move from the charmed circle of his presence, 'Oh, dear—I have offended!' And added, white teeth biting into a lip curved in half-horrified, half-humorous uncertainty: 'Not deeply, I hope?'

Jane fought to defend Dorabella's too clearly wounded pride. 'That must imply a depth of consequence which I think you will find is lacking.'

'Do you think so?' he said, suddenly more serious. 'Do you think that, in fact, there is not much depth to the—relationship?'

'What am I to reply?' thought Jane. Whatever she said, must be wrong from one point or the other. She compromised. 'I think a gentleman should recognise that where his feelings are light—so the lady's of necessity will be light also. The lady—if she is a lady, and Miss Mellowes is a lady—will see to that.'

He looked down at her. 'It is true that young ladies are remarkable creatures,' he said. 'A gentleman is not always under such self-command.'

Lady Mellowes wrote a formal acceptance of the Baines ball but regretted that Miss Bird would be unable to accompany her. Miss Bird received by return a crested note: 'Pray come! Mama insists that you shall! And so do I! Aurora Baines.' 'They are really very kind,' she said to Lady Mellowes, 'but I stand to my resolution.'

'I think you are right,' said Lady Mellowes, who, however, knew nothing of the warmth and fullness of the spoken invitation.

'Oh, certainly,' said Jane. And, besides, what could she have worn? But she thought of it all, the great ballroom, all white and gilt as Dorabella had described it to her, festooned with ropes of flowers beneath the glitter of the chandeliers: of the music and the dancing, of Dorabella's little feet flying, her little hand touching this hand and the next in the movements of the dance; of one hand meeting hers, retaining it: of blue eyes looking down, smiling, appealing, begging for mercy ... What man could resist her? she thought—so sweet and so pretty. Whatever he had meant by those last words he had spoken—what man could resist her when the petulance left her face and she looked up with those deep blue eyes smiling, with the tendrils of red-gold hair all escaped and framing her lovely little face—what man could resist her? And it was known all too well, it seemed, that he did not very easily resist; and himself was resisted never.

If she could have gone to the ball—would he have danced with her? With plain Jane Bird, governess and duenna to Miss Mellowes, the adorable?

Aurora Baines' note lay unfolded on the table. She could yet go. But ... 'Poor Cinderella,' she thought to herself, 'with not even a fairy godmother to come to your rescue!'

And there was a tap at the door and Bates, the ladies' maid, stood there with a large cardboard dress box. 'For you, Miss.'

'For me? It can't be for *me*, Miss Bates.' (Beware of that gap between heaven and earth!—Bates to everyone else, had best be Miss Bates to the governess.)

'It's addressed to you, Miss: there's no doubt about that.' Bates eyed it curiously. 'It looks like a dress, Miss Bird. Shall we not open it and see?'

A dress! A dress of glimmering blues and greens, close to the waist, the wide skirt flowing, moving, in a delicate rustle of taffetas. Blue and green, softly iridescent as the changing colours on the breast of a dove. A ball dress.

She went straight to Lady Mellowes. Lady Mellowes said: 'My dear, I assure you—I know nothing whatsoever about it.'

And Adorabella. 'Miss Bird—had I but thought of it myself! But I am so selfish and self-concerned, that I didn't.' And she added triumphantly, 'But now you *must* come to the ball!'

'My lady, of course, of course I could not accept such a gift.'

'How can you refuse, when you don't know who sent it?' said Adorabella.

'My dear,' said Lady Mellowes, 'you perhaps don't quite understand such matters.'

'But *Mama*! Cousin Hannah, come here, come in—see what someone has sent to Miss Bird. A ball dress!'

'Someone has sent it? Who has sent it?' said Miss Ferris.

'It's totally a mystery. Of course *you* know nothing about it?'

'Certainly not,' said Miss Ferris sharply. 'I should not approve of sending gowns to governesses. What could she use such a dress for?'

'It's sent to her so that she may come to Aurora Baines' ball.'

'I have no intention of going to the ball, Dorabella.'

'You must do so now! How hurt someone will be if you don't!'

A ball dress. Blue and green, iridescent as the breast of a dove. Callie had said that: Callie had described just such a dress, and said he should like to see her in it, that he would like to paint her. But Callie ... Callie could have no money for a dress like this, and, though he might wish her to have one, what was she to him?—what was he to her?—that he should provide it for her. Then ... ?

A memory flickered through her mind—of Callie saying, that if she were not careful she might make Adorabella jealous ...

As though she read the thought yet unborn, Dorabella said suddenly: 'Dominic!'

'What are you saying, Arabella?' said Miss Ferris, scandalised.

'Dominic was there when Callie described such a dress. It was he who began it all. He said—that he should like to see Miss Bird in a pretty dress, some such thing; then Callie suggested the fancy of the iridescent dove; and— yes, and Dominic said he knew where such shot taffetas was to be found...' And the look came to her face that had come to it then, as she had taken her cousin by the arm and walked away with him. 'You're not doing badly for yourself, Miss Bird,' she said. 'But a few brief weeks and the tutor, here, desires to paint you, my cousin is sending you ball dresses to be painted in; and don't think I haven't observed how my lover—my one-time lover— whispered to you, that day we came back from the shopping expedition; and how you whispered back to him!'

'Adorabella!' exclaimed Lady Mellowes, horrified, and 'Arabella!' cried Cousin Hannah, disgusted.

'I speak nothing but the truth. Let her but attract Lord Brunel, wooden leg and all, and I shall have no one left to me.'

'Adorabella—'

'My name is Arabella. Please call me by it,' said Dorabella, turning from the hand outflung in protestation.

'I will call you by it also,' said Lady Mellowes. 'Arabella, pray control yourself! You are doing Miss Bird a total injustice, that is obvious. But explain what you mean by such accusation.'

'Let her ask herself what I mean. She very well knows the answer.'

'Yes, I know the answer,' said Jane. She stood very white, stiff with rage and humiliation, all the long bitterness of thwarted girlhood happiness rising up, choking her. 'A young man spoke a kind word to me,' she said, 'threw me a kind word like a bone to a dog—and she, who all her

63

life has treated *him* like a dog, faithful, loyal, untiring in devotion, poor good Tray to be summoned or sent back to his kennel at a snap of her fingers—she who cares not two pins for his kindness and his compliments—must grudge a single friendly word, must grudge his even speaking as though I were a human being—let alone a woman. And the poor tutor, who also to her is hardly a human, "the old tutor", to be made a joke of, to be married off in humorous fantasy to the poor thing of a governess—even he mustn't speak a civil word, lest he offend against her jealous greed for admiration. And as for your precious lover, as you call him—' she turned upon Adorabella who now stood, white faced also, one hand clutching almost for support, at the tall back of her mother's chair '—all I did was to speak to him in your defence; for your sake, to preserve you from the demeaning effects of your own shameless jealousy, unconcealed and petulant. Do you think I want your lover? No thank you, Miss Mellowes! I will leave him to you—to you and to Miss Aurora Baines, and to a Miss Rutherford, I think the name was, and an Honourable Clarissa—not to mention a lady in Mayfair whom no gentleman may speak of with honour. And to . . .'

Her voice faltered. A foreign young lady, very beautiful, in a pretty little house behind a yellow painted door, she could not bring herself to mention. The blue-green dress lay across the arm of a chair. She let it lie. 'I will go and pack my things,' she said to Lady Mellowes. 'I won't accept the last humiliation of dismissal. At least it is I who give *you* notice. Perhaps someone would summon a hackney cab for me. I am leaving.'

Chapter 5

Upstairs in her room she flung herself down upon her bed—the white curtained four-poster in the flowery room that so short a time ago had seemed so pretty, so welcoming to the solitary stranger—and fell into a storm of weeping. There came, she thought, a light tap at her door but she ignored it. Later a tap came again; a note was pushed under the door. She ignored both. The tears subsided, she went to her wash-basin and bathed her face; but her head now ached violently, she was obliged to lie down again until the throbbing ended. Terror filled her heart. Easy to say that she would go, to send for a cab and drive away from it all for ever. But where go? The only home she had known in the past years, was now closed to her, occupied by strangers. A few pounds in the bank might see her through the next week while she sought for another position—sought without reference or recommendation for another position, not daring to return to the agency through which this one had been obtained, lest her reputation go there before her. And late afternoon was upon her, she had little ready money in her purse ... Moreover, the very practicalities of her going seemed overwhelming. To walk down the great staircase out to the waiting cab—perhaps to meet one or other of the family, Lady Mellowes reproachful of ill manners and ingratitude, Dorabella resentfully triumphant, Miss Ferris grimly glad to see her go ... To have to appeal to servants to manage the heavy trunk for her, who, behind her back would be gossiping and exclaiming at this sudden departure...

At this sudden departure. This leaving for ever of so much that had brought pleasure, had brought even something almost like happiness into a life so long deprived of either. To be leaving for ever all hope of seeing again that glance of forget-me-not-blue, that gleam that had said—surely had said?—to me, you are someone a little apart, you are somebody special...

But that gleam at least she might dismiss; that hope at least she might take both hands to and strangle. For Adorabella Mellowes also—that gleam! For Aurora Baines, for some unknown Miss Rutherford, for an Honourable Clarissa; for Mrs. Edgar Worcester with her conveniently absent husband: for a beautiful foreign young lady behind a yellow door ... 'What woman that sees him remains only "acquainted"?' That dream at least need present no more problem for her. That dream was ended.

A knock at the door: firmer this time. A voice said: 'It's Bates, Miss.'

The cab has arrived, she thought with horror. She's come to say that the cab has arrived, to help me down with my luggage. And she had not yet even begun to pack. She went to the door. 'I'm not quite ready, Miss Bates.'

Bates came into the room. She looked round, took in the rumpled bed, the tumbled hair, the white, tear-stained face. She said: 'There's no cause to hurry, Miss. Her ladyship wouldn't let you leave the house tonight, not if it was ever so.'

'Has a cab not been sent for?'

'Of course not, Miss. As if anyone would let you! Where would you go, this time of night? And for all we know, you have no money, no friends near enough to help you.' She was automatically straightening the bed as she spoke, plumping up the crushed pillows, turning back the covers, preparing it for the night. 'Let me take down your hair,

Miss, and brush it for you, it'll soothe you.' And she pushed the only half-protesting girl down on to a stool facing the dressing table and, expressionless, began to unpin the disordered hair, letting the soft hazel locks fall loosely about the drooping shoulders. 'Just sit easy and let me brush it, Miss; you'll find it very comforting. I always do this for her ladyship when she has the headache or feels upset and uneasy. Her ladyship gets upset, Miss, you know, more than you'd fancy from the way she has with her. She's so light and gay, she seems to carry so much happiness in her as though it were part of her—but underneath it all she's sensitive, her ladyship is, very sensitive and feeling. She can't bear any creature to be hurt or wounded. An injured bird by the roadside, that the carriage wheels have gone over ... "Oh, Bates," she'll say to me, "I can't get the thought out of my head! Poor little things that should be so free and pretty, singing away so blithely..." That's a word of her ladyship's ,"singing away so blithely", she'll say to me. I didn't know what it meant at first but now I've taken care to discover; and indeed, I sometimes think it applies to her ladyship herself. Only underneath the blithelyness—well, as I say, her heart's so kind and filled with pity.' The brush moved rhythmically through the long, soft hair. ' "Go up to that poor child, Bates," she says to me,' said Bates, not altering at all the tone of her voice, ' "and see how she's doing. Make her let you brush her hair for her; it's always so lovely and soothing..." '

'Yes. She's very kind and thoughtful,' said Jane, dully. She moved her head away from the restraining hands. 'Thank you, Miss Bates. I'm much better now. Thank you.'

'There's a note here for you, pushed under the door,' said Bates. 'You haven't opened it.'

'I don't want to open any notes. If I could just ... Yes, I think it would be best if I might just stay here for tonight, Miss Bates, after all; and then, if you'd be so kind as to see to it personally, not troubling anybody else about it—

I could take a cab and go away quietly before they're all stirring...'

'The note is from Miss Arabella,' said Bates, turning it over in her hands.

'I don't want to open any notes. I don't want any more to do with any of it. I don't know,' said Jane, putting her hand to her burning forehead, 'whether I've behaved badly or others have behaved badly. It doesn't matter now; I only wish to go away and to do so quietly without making any disturbance.'

'You don't surely think, Miss, that her ladyship would let you go like that—without a word?'

'I think there've been enough words,' said Jane. 'What's the use of any more? I shall be leaving anyway. I could apologise, but of what use at this stage are apologies?'

'I think in fact, Miss, that the apologies may come from Miss Arabella,' said Bates in her toneless voice; and held out the note again.

'Well, I want no apologies—I don't know where I am, whether I've been in the right or in the wrong; but I lost my temper, I was exceedingly rude and I should accept no apologies. And Miss Mellowes lost *her* temper and was rude to *me*—and I want no apologies.' She took the note from the maid's hand; a fire burned, as ever in that comfortable room. She tossed the unopened envelope into it. 'All I want is to leave here,' she said.

'Her ladyship will wish to see you, Miss Bird,' said Bates.

'I won't see her. Please let me not have the shame of sitting here behind a locked door and refusing to see her. But I will *not* see her. I won't see her or Miss Arabella, I certainly won't see Miss Ferris.' She struck her hand against her forehead, sick with desperation. 'If I could have been gone by now, I should have. Can they not let me alone? I'll be gone tomorrow. I will not see anyone.'

Bates left the room; quiet, unemotional, colourless. She returned in a short time with a tray of food and a glass of wine. 'I am to see, Miss, that you drink the wine at least.'

Jane took the glass with an ill grace and drained it. 'There then!' she said, dumping it back on the tray again.

'And her ladyship asks once more ... She tells me to put it this way,' said Bates, carefully. 'That there is no need for you to leave here unless you insist upon it; and she asks you—she begs you, Miss, to see her.' And now a slight tremor did come into Bates' expressionless voice. 'Her ladyship using that word to you, Miss Bird—she begs you to see her.'

'Please thank her. Please say that I'm grateful, she makes me humble, using such a word to me. But please ask her to let me go in peace. I won't see anyone.'

Bates left. Jane dragged her trunk out of its corner and began a desultory packing. Downstairs across the arm of a drawing-room chair—did the shimmering blue-green dress still lie where she had thrown it? That dress—first cause of all these new miseries! And yet ... Someone had sent it to her. Someone in all this aridity of governessing, had cared enough to plan it, to have it made for her, to send it. She thought for a moment of the tall figure and the fair head and the brilliant blue eyes. Would *he* have liked to see her in the blue-green dress...?

Steps outside again; but a heavier footfall than Bates', more positive. A voice called: 'Miss Bird! Open the door, I wish to speak to you.' Miss Ferris. Jane made no reply.

'Miss Bird!' The door handle rattled. 'Let me in!' And as again Jane made no answer, she called more sharply: 'Why don't you reply? Are you ill?' A moment more of silence. 'Very well, then—I have a key and I must come in and see to you.' Before Jane could cry out in repudiation, the key had turned and Miss Ferris came into the room.

'I don't wish to see anyone,' said Jane. 'Please go away!'

For answer, Miss Ferris walked across the room, stooped and picked out of the ashes of the fire, the half-consumed note which Jane had earlier flung there. 'What's this? This looks like Arabella's handwriting.'

'A letter was pushed under the door,' said Jane. 'I threw it into the fire, unread.'

Miss Ferris was delicately smoothing out the remaining scorched scrap of paper. She read out: ' "I am bitterly..." The rest is burned away; but one can suppose it to have been, "I am bitterly sorry" or "bitterly ashamed". And, "If you can..." If you can forgive me, I suppose she intended. And again, "...thoughtless and conceited. You are quite right." ' She folded the scrap and put it aside on the dressing table. 'An apology, apparently. And, it would seem, rather generous. It would have been more generous in *you*, at least to have read it.'

Jane rested back, wearily, on the edge of the high mattress, one arm about the upright of the draped four-poster bed. 'How could I know it would not have been simply more—insults?'

Miss Ferris looked at her almost scornfully. 'Do you really think Arabella a girl to sit down and in cold blood write insults.'

'Very well, then, reproaches: for my rudeness, if you will, which was certainly rudeness.'

'It is an apology,' said Miss Ferris. She went over and sat on the edge of the high window-seat, very handsome in her dark dress against the bright curtains. 'It is an apology and you very well knew it was that. But you are obdurate in your hurt pride. Well—that I understand. You were accused and insulted; and while you were not in a position to defend yourself. Though I must concede that you did defend yourself—somewhat too well.'

'I think it's—ignoble—for people to insult their inferiors.'

'I think so too,' said Miss Ferris. She indicated the scrap of paper. 'And so, evidently, does Arabella.'

'And unpardonable for their inferiors to insult them in return.'

'In that respect, she seems to disagree with you. To ask

for pardon, is to imply one's own forgiveness.'

What had she come here for? Jane wondered—this cold, haughty woman with her direct, cool, sensible—almost sensitive—answers. She said: 'What is the use of discussion? The sooner you leave me, the sooner I may continue with my preparations and go away from here forever.'

'Lady Mellowes has sent me to talk some sense into you. Why should you be so determined not to stay?'

Jane shook her weary head. 'Stay on here? After what has passed? Nobody could wish it. I wouldn't wish it myself. Words were spoken that can never be forgotten.'

'A spoilt little miss spat out like a vicious kitten, in her jealousy. A young woman, not very much older, has answered in like kind. The whole thing may be forgotten in a moment, if you are generous.' And she pointed again to the paper. 'A much younger, less disciplined girl has excelled you in that.'

'Miss Ferris,' said Jane, 'you were there, you heard what was said. You heard me accused of—of trying to appropriate Miss Mellowes' admirers. A vulgar, scheming, mere nobody of a governess, coming in here, insinuating herself into the family, in the hopes of finding herself a husband, I suppose (but Miss Mellowes has catered for that already; another has been discovered so low that he is not too good for me as I, God knows, couldn't be too good for him!)—flirting and ogling to attract attention to myself and away from her...'

But Miss Ferris was not listening. She said sharply: 'Who has been "discovered"?'

'Oh, have no fear!—it's only the poor tutor, "Dommie's old tutor", good enough for me as I am good enough for him; and neither of us higher than a couple of pet dogs that may be paired off for the mating—'

'Callie?' said Miss Ferris, incredulous. She asked on an odd note of urgency: 'Does *he* know anything of this?'

'Good heavens!' said Jane. 'Is even he to be denied me?

71

But have no fear—he speaks to me civilly, even kindly when we meet. I suppose he is not to do less?—but at least he does no more.' However much she might scheme and ogle, she added, bitterly.

'Now, now,' said Miss Ferris, 'don't lose your temper again!' But she spoke now with less chill, almost kindly reasoning with her. 'You know very well in your heart that Arabella meant no such thing. It's true that you have been shamed and—wounded; there is no need, however, to be quite so determined to feel injured. A silly, spoilt thoughtless girl is piqued because she fancies a moment's abstraction on the part of one who has always been her slave alone—and Dominic has been that since her child-hood. But you know very well that she would never have had such ugly thoughts as you suggest: and for the rest, it is nothing to do with your position; she would have spoken as she did to the highest in the land.'

'If I had been the highest in the land, she might have done so. As I am the lowest, she takes a despicable ad-vantage.'

'She is not a girl to take despicable advantages,' said Miss Ferris, coldly again. 'She is spoilt and wilful; I know that, if no one else does. And what she said was out-rageous. But at least she paid you the compliment of for-getting that you were what you describe as "the lowest". She spoke to you, simply quarrelling, as with an equal.' She looked Jane up and down, coolly; almost taunting her, it seemed, into rationality. 'We must beware,' she suggested in her cold voice, 'of *too* much self pity.'

Jane rested her weary forehead against the polished wood of the bed-post. Slow tears welled up and crept down her pale cheeks. 'Of course.' She turned away, scrubbing at her eyes with an already damp handkerchief. She said despairingly: 'What does it all matter? Why don't you just let me go?'

Miss Ferris appeared to lose patience. 'Now come, Miss Bird, pull yourself together! The world has not come to an end! And nor has the world of Robinsford for you, unless you're so foolish as to force it to do so. A silly girl burst out at you in a fit of spite and jealousy. What of it? She doesn't believe her own accusations, and they're not true. Unless . . .' She looked Jane coolly up and down again. 'I've observed that that other one—the secretary, Havering —extends his flirtations towards you; he denies them to no woman, I suspect. And as to a little essay in that quarter—nothing but good might come of that. You need be in no danger; you are mercifully fore-warned of the gentleman's long list of conquests; and in the certain knowledge that his attentions to a young woman of no fortune are not likely to be serious. Indeed, you might do the family a great service, in rescuing Arabella from his toils.'

'For the benefit of Lord Brunel?' said Jane coldly. So this was where all this salutary advice had been leading! The spider was to be allured away from the precious little family fly.

'No one forces Arabella,' said Miss Ferris, calmly. 'That such a marriage would suit the family's condition, nobody denies; but nothing suggests that it would be an unwise or unhappy one. Meanwhile, however, all is endangered by her infatuation with this—this untimely admirer. A professional heart-breaker.'

'Miss Aurora Baines and half a dozen others remain to distract him,' said Jane bitterly, 'without your having recourse to a defenceless governess as counter-attraction.'

'The governess may be amply defended by prior knowledge of his reputation.' But she lifted her head and looked at Jane keenly. 'It by no means is true, that you also—?'

Jane interrupted her, getting up off the bed. She said sharply: 'Well—stay or go, Madam, one thing is certain. The governess has yet her poor rags of pride and will play no such games for the protection of any young lady. Look to her yourselves. For the rest, I have no pretensions to Miss Mellowes' admirers. Mr. Dominic Mellowes seeks to please the custodian of the goods he covets—a phrase you yourself taught me; and as for the tutor...' She recollected their talk as they had strolled back from the stables to the Great House. 'The tutor perhaps does the same.'

'What do you mean?' said Miss Ferris, in that oddly urgent, sharp tone again.

'He once warned me,' said Jane, 'of the bitterness of ever presuming to aspire above one's situation. He seemed to speak from his own experience.'

'Well—very well,' said Miss Ferris, shrugging it off. But for the second time her attitude seemed subtly to change, to grow to something more of warmth. 'Come then, Miss Bird! No one asks you in fact to sacrifice your feelings to our family necessities. For the rest—be magnanimous, for so we shall consider it. Forget this childish business—for which there has, I assure you, been much almost equally childish remorse. Go to bed now, sleep soundly; and tomorrow let Lady Mellowes talk to you, and your pupil make you suitably humble apology; and don't, through false pride, drive away such good and kind friends as you have found here.' She rose and went to the door. 'I will send Bates to you; and will go down now and tell her ladyship that my mission is accomplished.' She gave the words only a hint of a question mark; and in a moment was gone.

Jane stood silently and watched her go. Bates came to her with a glass of hot milk, stirred with honey. 'Go to bed now, Miss. Sleep is a comfort and you'll find it so.' She laid out the soft lawn nightgown on the bed, folded back, ready to slip into. At the door, she turned. 'No cabs are to be sent for, Miss,' she said. 'Her ladyship hopes to see you at ten o'clock in her boudoir. She bids you sleep late, and keep to your room until then.' She went out; but before she closed the door behind her, popped her head back in again. 'We all love our young lady, Miss Bird,' she said. 'But into each life a little rain must fall; and perhaps a very small shower will really have done no harm, will it?'

*　　*　　*

74

Lady Mellowes, the little Dowager, rose up out of her chair. She wore a morning gown, all muslin and ribbons and lace, her fair hair not yet come under the elaborate dressing which it must receive before she ventured forth for the day. She held out a hand, the froth of lace falling back against her white, rounded arm. 'Miss Bird—you are kind to come!' And she leaned forward and gave Jane's cheek a little, gentle kiss. 'May we forget all our troubles and start our happy life again?'

'I have to apologise to your ladyship—'

'No, you have not. Let us forget all apologies.'

'Your ladyship is very kind—'

'Well, no, on balance it will be you who are kind to do so.' And she put out her hand and lifted up the downcast face. 'Come—put back that radiance that is not only in the shimmery silk of your dress! Allow me to send for my erring daughter and, of your generosity, accept her back into your good graces, where I know she once had her little place From there, we can continue as before. No one knows anything of this except ourselves—you and I and Arabella, and Miss Ferris, of course. The staff is aware, no doubt, that there's been some trouble, that you had given us your notice and wished to depart; that we have been at great pains to persuade you to alter your mind. No one else in the world knows what was said, or shall know. It is something, I think, that you in your quiet way have made yourself in this short time so felt here, that I do believe they are all—not knowing the details—rather on your side than on ours!' She smiled again. 'Now—may I send for the sinner?' And as Jane stood silent, defeated, she added: 'And then we want to see you try on your beautiful dress.'

Dorabella came in, unwontedly hesitant; the shimmering dress over her arm. She glanced at her mother enquiringly; seemed reassured by what she saw, came across to Jane and, folding the dress over the back of a chair, put her arms round her and laid her soft, satiny,

75

childish cheek against hers. 'We're not to speak of forgiveness,' she said. 'But may we be friends again?' And stood
back and looked into her face and said, as her mother had
said: 'Come—be your sweet, kind, smiling self again, Miss
Radiant Dove!'

'Who can resist any of you?' said Jane; and for the
first time smiled.

'Now of course you'll have to come to the dance,' said
Adorabella, and picked up the blue-green dress.

It was very well for them—for all of the family, so secure
in their position of superiority, of rightness and ease. But
how should she again face those whom she was supposed,
however slightly, to have 'attracted'? Lady Mellowes had
said that they were ignorant—that all the rest of their
little world was ignorant—of accusation and counter-
accusation; of the cause of the trouble that had arisen so
swiftly, been so comparatively swiftly extinguished—at
the Dower House. But how comport herself with these
gentlemen under the eyes of those who were aware of what
had been? Even in her renewal of peace and happiness
under the kindliness of those about her—she sometimes
wished that her first intention had been carried out;
that she were by now away, entering perhaps upon some
other 'servitude' where, though conditions might be less
delightful, her pupils would be of an age where a gentleman might speak a civil good-day to the governess without
evoking storms of rage and tears.

On the other hand...

On the other hand—had not those blue eyes shone for
her with an especial shining? And light of heart he
might be, on fortune bent he might be—but she had not
been so rich in kind glances but that one, so piercing in
its sweetness, should not be a treasure hugged to her secret
heart—perhaps for all her secret life.

'I couldn't go,' she thought; 'not while I might hope for
another such look as that.' Meaningless, casual, barely

conscious, perhaps; but a thirsty man must crave even the snowflake that in a moment melted away in his hand.

Insincere? Meaningless? 'I am a penniless nobody,' she thought. 'If he didn't mean it, why should he trouble to smile with such eyes at *me*?'

And the notion flickered in and out of her mind again. Not Lady Mellowes. Not Dorabella. Not old Lady Mellowes up at the Great House who would not have acted without at least consulting the Dowager. Not Dominic. Not Callie. Who else, then, had known of Callie's vision of that gown, the colour of a pigeon's breast?

Callie had spoken of it when they came back from the visit to the stables. Callie had described the dress. And *he* had been there: he with all his love of the arts, of beauty, of colour—he had been there.

Had Richard Havering also, wished to see her wear an iridescent blue-green dress?

Callie came riding with them the following day. He had brought down the stout little dapple-grey, Honeycomb— with orders to make sure that it would not be more suitable for Miss Bird than the bay, Aldebaran. 'We'll go down by the water meadows,' said Adorabella. 'Miss Bird hasn't yet ridden that way.' Miss Bird up to now had ridden chiefly along the bridle path to where the beech tree marked the end of that way which Richard Havering had been wont to take, in hopes of an 'accidental' meeting. But Richard rode no more that way. 'I wonder,' thought Jane, 'if he regrets the discovery of those few black stitches in the tapestry which keep his nose so closely to Sir Dermot's grindstone?' She had searched out the mark but it made no sense to her at all. Three or four stitches in a perpendicular row; and that was all.

Across the river Dominic appeared, mounted on a fine chestnut, taller and heavier than Dorabella's pretty little Majority. A truly chance meeting. He was making his rounds of the estate. Dorabella gee-upped her little horse and crossed the bridge to join him, cantering with him easily over the flat meadow land. Jane, left behind, came to a resolution. 'Mr. Carrell—'

'Callie,' he corrected. 'I am Callie to all my friends.'

'I've been here so short a time. May I already call you a friend?'

'You may call me Callie at any rate,' he said, laughing. 'In fact you must. I shan't answer unless you do.'

'Will that be—correct? Before the family, I mean?—in my position.'

'Why, good gracious!' he said, '—they have us married off already—didn't you know? Who may call me by my familiar name, if not my future wife?' She flushed up at too recent recollections and he, ignorant of them, supposed himself to have offended her. 'Forgive me, I'm only teasing. They've been arranging marriages for me for the past hundred years; every new young lady who comes to "governess" Dorabella—and they have been legion: none before have been of your calibre, my dear Miss Dove!—has been apportioned to me: though none I assure you,' he added, laughingly bowing as he rode, 'with so much hope of success!' And riding close, he put out a hand to her. 'It is all in fun; don't take offence at it. Let us be friends!' His left hand on the reins, he held out his right.

She took it: smiled back at him. 'Then as a friend, I will confide in you. You've heard of the mysterious arrival of this beautiful dress?'

'Cast no suspicious eye in my direction, my dear Miss Dove! With all the good will in the world, with all the desire in the world to see your charms done so much justice to—I could no more afford the luxury of such a surprise gift, than fly.'

'I wonder if surprise gifts are always the boon they set out to be? Sometimes the anxiety as to the donor is as painful as the gift is delightful.'

'I agree with you. Still, someone *has* wished to delight

you. To someone,' he said, not looking at her, 'you are not just a governess.'

'On the contrary. It is because I am a governess. No one would send Miss Mellowes a gift of this nature.'

'Miss Mellowes has all the dresses her heart could desire.'

'No one would send her any such gift. Her own cousin begs permission of Mama, before he even dares offer the chestnut pony.'

The stolid little grey took no handling; one might converse without other interruption. He said: 'You see yourself only in the mirror of your—dependence.'

'I have been dependent before,' she said. 'But never a servant.'

'Since you *are* a servant, as you choose to call it—had you not better make the best of it, and be happy?'

She said: 'You imply a reproach.'

'I think you are—if you will forgive me—missish on the subject. And I think that, in these circumstances, that is ungrateful.'

'Yes,' she said, humbled. 'I will try to forget it.'

'But as to the dress—someone, I repeat, looks upon you as—well, we will say this, in deference to your determination to be belittled—as not only a governess but as a person; a person to be pleased, flattered, made happy, a person to look beautiful: a person to go to a ball—'

'Of course I shall not go to the ball!'

'—on equal terms with the other pretty ladies there.'

'I shouldn't go on equal terms with the ladies, however I might be got up to look like one.'

'You *are* a lady,' he said. 'And a very pretty lady. And in that dress, will be a very beautiful lady; I think you hardly know, yourself, how beautiful. As beautiful a lady, I daresay, as any at the ball.'

' "Who can be that beautiful young lady my noble son is dancing with?" "Why, dear Duchess, a Miss Jane Bird, paid governess to Miss Mellowes of Robinsford..." '

'Few duchesses are to be met with, chez Baines,' said

Callie, patiently. 'And a great many people no grander, I assure you, than Miss Mellowes' governess.' And he bowed, grinning. 'After all, Mr. Vincent Carrell, erstwhile tutor to Mr. Dominic Mellowes, will be there; and you can hardly get much lower than that. I have Miss Hannah Ferris's word for it.' But alas!—he added, he could not plead guilty to having sent Miss Mellowes' governess a ball gown.

No one at the Dower House.

No one at the Great House.

Unless...

But she did not dare to sound him as to that 'unless'. Even to herself, hardly dared put the possibility into words.

Yet there was no one else.

Conversation with Dominic was more difficult; both she and Dorabella were somewhat ill at ease, Dorabella staying back, urging them into exchange of civilities, Jane stiff and embarrassed. A little to her horror, however, he seemed to look upon her with a particular attentiveness, even more so than at the time of the visit to the stables. The secret of the gift of the dress had been revealed to him, in an endeavour to discover the donor; and he was much intrigued by it, full of compliments as to her coming appearance in it. 'We shall see you wear it at Miss Baines' party on Thursday evening?'

'Of course I shan't go there. It's very kind of everybody but it's out of the question.'

His face fell. 'But then we shan't see you in the dress!'

'And I shall refuse to paint you in it,' declared Callie. 'I couldn't paint a young lady in a dress which hadn't at least been worn to a ball.'

Now the spring sunshine was gone and it threatened rain; but a lovely light lay across the green meadows with their thread of grey-green water between. They stood in a little knot, their horses restlessly moving, hands light on the controlling reins. Dominic said: 'And what shall I do with the bouquet already ordered for you?—flowers from the hot-house, of pale pearl and pink, the colour of the dove's bill, as Aurora Baines suggested. I had set my heart on your carrying them—with my compliments.' He said a trifle off-handedly to Dorabella: 'One is ordered for you, also, of course: your mother tells me you will wear your lovely pale pink dress with the roses.'

'I could not possibly accept,' said Jane, unhappily.

'Do you mean my flowers? But you must! My mother has sought out her flower-holder, of mother-of-pearl. She wishes you to have it as a small gift for this—your first?—great ball.'

'Her flower-holder: the silver and pearl? Oh, Dominic, I have always coveted that!'

'You have half a dozen of your own, Dorabella. Let Miss Dove have her *one*.'

'"Miss Dove!"' said Dorabella, divided between chagrin and laughter. But the laughter won. 'Oh, dear Miss Dove, my little, quiet, undemanding dove—yes, of course you shall have the holder; I wouldn't grudge it to you if it were diamonds and gold.'

'I knew you wouldn't—when I suggested to my mother that she make the gift,' said Dominic, innocently.

'*You* asked? Then the suggestion came from—?'

'It came from me, Dorabella,' said Callie swiftly. 'I wanted Miss Bird to carry such flowers to go with her dress; and of course I'm not master of the hot-houses like his young lordship here. The rest followed.' He smiled at her reassuringly; but all of them present knew that he told a fib.

You could see the small hands tighten on the rein, the eyes begin to flash, the soft lips firm into a narrow line; but she controlled herself. 'I think it's a lovely idea. And to make all perfect,' she said to Jane, and forced her eyes to smiling though her mouth now trembled a little, 'I shall give you my pearl-handled fan to go with the holder.'

'Why, Dorabella, *I* gave you—'

'But won't grudge my passing it on—as it's to Miss Dove?' said Adorabella sweetly.

Jane turned Honeycombe's head with something too much like a jerk, and started away. 'I'm sorry,' she said as Callie caught up with her. 'She pulled suddenly on the bit and started without me.'

'Oh, certainly,' said Callie solemnly. 'A savage beast, impossible of control. We must get you back on to Aldebaran before you're carried home on a gate.' And he plunged two fingers into a pocket. 'Where all else are so generous,' he said, 'can your chosen husband lag so far behind?' He held out to her a small flat piece of card. 'It cost nothing—like Dommie's flowers, which therefore you can't refuse—and *un*like Dommie's flowers, you can't take it to the ball with you. But it will be perhaps—a remembrance of it.'

A sketch—very light, very airy-fairy, almost fantastical: a sketch in fine pen and ink with a wash of water-colour...

A young girl dancing; pointed in a half turn, so that she seemed almost in the very act of movement. A hand held out to an unseen partner ... Small, neat hazel head with only a single curl falling softly forward over the turning shoulder, caught in a cluster of pale, waxy flowers: close bodice—swirl of skirt, shimmering, shining in a stipple of iridescent green and blue. The figure of a young girl, dancing: of Jane Bird dancing, with upturned, smiling, rapturous, untroubled face.

'You see, you must go,' he said. 'Or it won't come true.'

Nevertheless, thought Jane, I shall not go. To have everyone watching her dance in the iridescent dress, to have one watching who had secretly sent it ... Would *he* be watching her? Would he be watching her, exulting in it?— thinking to himself that now he had snared the poor dove who so unthinkingly accepted and wore the gift *he* had sent? Was it so that a rake would set his innocent-seeming traps?—to protest some day when a time came that suited him. After all—you accepted the gift of a dress from me...

They had each so kindly, so charmingly, offered her gifts: had the dress been his?

I shall not go, she thought. I could not go.

Dorabella had left Dominic and cantered ahead to catch up with them. Jane entered upon lame explanations of her pony's sudden taking off. Dorabella hardly heard her. 'A button has come loose on my habit. Callie, dear—a moment alone with Miss Bird?' As Callie dropped back and joined Dominic she said: 'It isn't a button at all. It is that ... Miss Dove, do you see—those two riders going up the hill towards the Great House? It is my uncle—with *him!*'

So lately had she been thinking of him with just that emphasis in her own mind, that Jane was almost startled. She controlled herself however to say coolly: 'By him, do you mean Mr. Richard Havering?'

'But of course. Now, Miss Dove, my dearest Miss Dove, my dear little shining Miss Dove—do this for me! Accept that we go up to the House for refreshment before returning to Mama. Who knows but that he may be with my aunt? I suppose at least at home, my uncle and he emerge sometimes from their den.'

'Dorabella, I think it is not for a lady to—to pursue a gentleman...'

'Whom do I pursue? I ask only to take a glass of cordial with my own aunt, before continuing the arduous journey all that way, a full quarter of a mile downhill for home!' She put on her pretty little pouting, pleading face. 'Come—I was nice to you about Dommie's flowers!'

'I shan't accept his flowers, my dear, though I think he was being only thoughtful and kind to one in my position.'

'You and your "position"! He was thoughtful and kind because he *is* kind—and because he thinks of you.'

They had turned their horses and now walked them

slowly forward. 'Dorabella—shall we not speak of this matter just once more? I covet, I accept, no attention from any of your—acquaintance. If I am to be plagued with such suspicions, I must go away.'

'I don't suspect you. You can't help it if gentlemen admire you.'

'No one admires me, you foolish girl! How could they, when *you* are by, with all your little charms and graces. I am hardly a person to them, just a small grey dove who has in her care—what have I in my care?—a bird of bright plumage, a little golden bird, all singing and sunshine. Don't grudge me a pleasant word, a kind glance—you who have so much; but don't, either, misunderstand that it is all no more than I say: a kind glance and a pleasant word, a few crumbs from the courtesy of generous hearts, for the inoffensive dove.'

'I have known the dove turn to an eagle in her day,' said Dorabella, laughing. 'I think she is not altogether so much a dove as we give her credit for. And on Thursday night we shall see her in her true feathers; and then and at any other time, she's welcome to all who come. All except one. Or all except two, perhaps; I'm too much accustomed to my Dommie's devotion to find myself comfortable if I think he begins to fail in it. Dominic is mine. The rest you may have—except one.'

'Well, for my part I thank you for this dispensing of gentlemen's favours. But as to your going to the Great House—my dear, I'm sorry, but...'

'Don't trouble yourself any further with your duties as duenna,' said Dorabella, eyes dancing. 'The Great House is coming to me!'

For he had seen them, spoken a word to Sir Dermot and left him; and was riding back down the hill towards them.

Dorabella touched up the little chestnut and trotted forward to meet him. Jane, unable to bring herself to do the same, saw how the eager, pretty face was lifted up to his, the little hand held out, palm upturned: saw the quick, almost furtive kiss on the inside wrist that seemed to be some small private custom, the little intimate kiss of a forbidden love. He seemed to be speaking to her earnestly, looking down into her flushed face. ('If he would ever so speak to me!' thought Jane. 'If he would ever so look down into my eyes with that look that says, You are all the world to me...!')

And yet ... Had he not, even for her, that special look, that gleam of blue? Not entirely imagination, not all just nothing but the wishful thought. Though she might call it flirtatious, even Miss Ferris had recognised that gleam. She avoided it, not looking into his face as she rode up to them, not hastening her horse nor too obviously slowing it down. 'Miss Bird—I have been saying to Miss Mellowes that it's too long since we all met.'

'Miss Dove,' corrected Dorabella, all alight with happiness. 'That's what we all call her now, Miss Dove!'

And the blue gleam came. He looked into her eyes. 'A charming name! For what, after all, is a dove? A little, quiet bird with yet an iridescent sheen to its smooth grey feathers, as Callie described it the other day; lovelier than all the brilliance of your vulgar, showy cockatoo; and a bright look in its quick, alert eye, and the lovely, cooing, murmuring voice...' He seemed to start almost out of an abstraction. He bowed in his saddle to Adorabella: 'You will always think of the *mot juste*,' he said. 'You have always the exactly right touch.'

'Miss Shining Dove,' said Adorabella, having been ready to take umbrage, perhaps, now mollified at having the compliment neatly turned in her favour.

'Do you ride up to the house? Lady Mellowes will be ready with refreshments, I'm sure. She was in the morning room when we left her, watching as you rode down by the water-meadows.' He said, as they turned their horses and started up the hill, Callie and Dominic following behind them: 'I've been telling Miss Mellowes, Miss Dove, that I've been every moment of my time at Sir

85

Dermot's call. We can't unravel the mystery of the mark in the tapestry; a small mystery, I feel sure, but while it continues to puzzle us, we can't let it rest.'

Lady Mellowes was in the morning room, sure enough, with coffee and cordials and plates of sweet cakes and fruit. She accepted Jane's curtseyed greeting with a friendly smile. 'I am particularly delighted to see you, Miss Bird.'

'We are all to call her Miss Dove,' said Dorabella, pleased with her latest fancy. 'Mr. Havering thinks it suits her down to a T.'

Lady Mellowes turned upon him a long, ironical look; glanced briefly at Jane. 'Well, then, Miss Dove,' she said, 'have you heard that I have a little gift for you?'

'Your ladyship is very kind,' said Jane, 'very, very kind. But—'

'We are all giving her presents,' said Dorabella eagerly. 'Dominic is arranging for her flowers, I've promised her my mother-of-pearl fan. Dominic gave it to me originally but he is allowing me to offer it, aren't you, Dommie?'

'If *you* are not to keep it,' said Dominic, 'I can think of no one whom it would more grace than our Miss Dove.'

Richard Havering looked up sharply; bent his head again. What did that look say? wondered Jane, intercepting it, her heart racing. Did it not say, What is this sudden gallantry? No other man shall give presents to her but I?

'Miss Dove will not accept it, however,' she said. 'Though with all my thanks for the thought, Adorabella. I shan't need it; nor, my lady, with my grateful, grateful thanks for your goodness—shall I need the pearl holder for the flowers. I have said so steadily and all along and I say it again: I shall not go to the ball.'

He raised his head again; and the long, blue look pierced her heart as though it had been an arrow fired from his own. He said: 'Oh, but you *must* go!'

A tiny shock ran round the little group; a tiny shock of almost unconscious recognition. As though to cover it, as though to counteract the impression he might have given, he said immediately: 'Why else have you your beautiful dress?'

(To dance with him! To touch his fingers, to feel his hand at my waist, to look up into his eyes! To dance with you, my love!) But she said again, 'I couldn't go.'

'But we're all giving you our presents,' said Adorabella, almost wailing. 'Of course you must go. Your dress and your flowers and your fan ... And Mama will give you some pretty trinket, I know she will; she won't lag behind when we're all petting you with our gifts. It will be—ungracious—if you won't go.'

'You were going to say "ungrateful",' said Jane. 'And indeed I'm not. But in this dress—sent by some unknown person—how could I go? The suspicions, the speculation —in some quarter unknown to me, perhaps, the triumph! You know that I couldn't wear the dress. You know that I couldn't go.'

Richard Havering stood up. He spoke very lightly now, no blue glance darted, he might have been lightly sparring with any circle of casual acquaintance. He said: 'I have not yet come forward with *my* offering to Miss Bird. But I have something for her.' He patted his pocket. 'And when I have given it...' He looked round him, gaily challenging. 'Who will wager with me that our Miss Dove will not, after all, go to the ball?'

'A golden sovereign,' said Dominic Mellowes, as lightly. 'If she won't go so that she may carry my flowers why should she be persuaded by any bribe *you* may offer?'

'And I a sovereign also,' said Lady Mellowes. 'What young lady could accede to anything else, who resists my pearl and silver flower-holder?'

'And I a half-sovereign,' said Callie, 'since more is beyond me. For if she can resist *my* offering—which you none of you have seen and shall not—yet: why then, she won't go to the ball.'

'I'll wager the first dance,' said Adorabella. 'Which I

trust will be more precious than a sovereign, to any gentleman.'

Jane stood petrified; turned to stone, dreading some new embarrassment, some new inward agony. She stammered: 'I want nothing from anyone. Why should I be so—so cajoled?—I had almost said so bullied, but I know how kind you all are—into going where I don't wish to go, where it will all be confusion and shame for me...?' And the big room with its silk-panelled walls, its white wood and gilding, its great windows looking down over the green meadows, the darkling blue of the watery sky— the little group, sitting upright on the brocaded, spindle-legged chairs, the table with its silver and white napery, its heaped dish of peaches and grapes—all dissolved for a moment into a haze of tears unshed. 'Pray, pray, press me no more!' she said.

He put two long white fingers into the side pocket of his coat and produced an envelope, small, square and sealed. On it in a large flourishing, not very well formed hand was her name: Miss Bird.

My dear Miss Bird,
    I fear dreadfully that I may have offended you. I hope not, with all my heart. Perhaps what I did was foolish; I did not consult Mama who was absent from home, and she says now that I lacked tactfulness. I believe that Mr. Havering also thinks this too. But I wanted you so much to come to my ball and I guessed that you might have no dress. And that morning at the Great House Mr. Carrell described the dress he would paint you in if he could and that such a material was obtainable, and that day at Dashwood's Emporium, I studied your size and form and now you will know what I refer to, dear Miss Bird. Forgive me if I have erred. Do not misunderstand me if I confide to you that I also know something of what your feelings must too often be. My Papa is rich, but we have no pretensions

to Birth or to any equality with most of our acquaint-ance since we came here to The Towers. We feel it to be of no real importance that some will not know us, but sometimes a deliberate slight will wound or a word of contempt or a sneer. Our skins are not thick because the blood that flows beneath them is not so blue as some. Nor is your skin thick, I know, and so I feel that you may sometimes feel your position onerous, a real lady as you are and looking the lady, every inch. And so—I wanted you to come to my ball, to be dressed as a lady should be dressed, which all my fine clothes will not ever make *me* look, I know, though I make no great complaint of that for I am happy and safe in a thousand other ways. Dear Miss Bird—if I have discommoded you by my thoughtlessness in sending the dress without my name attached (but I thought you might not accept it if you knew that it came from one, almost a stranger) if I have embarrassed and perhaps distressed you as Mr. Havering seems to hint—then I beg you truly, to for-give me, and to show your forgiveness by wearing the gift as I meant it to be worn. Mama joins with me in dismay that my thought (which I have now of course confessed to her) may have caused you pain, and in the earnest hope that we shall see you on Thursday, in all your loveliness.

I am,

Yours with kindest regards,

Aurora Baines.

Chapter 6

Miss Ferris by no means approved Jane's going to the ball. 'You are inconsistent, Cousin Hannah. You're Mama's companion but won't go because you're too grand; and Miss Dove is *my* companion but may not go because she's too humble. Which way would you have it?'

'I am of the Family, Arabella. And as one of the Family I decline to go to that vulgar woman's house.'

'If it's good enough for Mama to go to—?'

'Lady Mellowes from the Great House does not go.'

'Good heavens, what would Aunt Mellowes do, hopping about at a ball with her poor lame leg? As well send your Lord Brunel; a fine pair they'd make together!' Dorabella seized up the poker, held it stiffly against one leg and reeled round the room in a ludicrous scramble, so that Jane could scarcely contain her laughter. 'At any rate, Mama goes and I go—and Miss Dove comes with us.'

'In her borrowed plumes,' said Cousin Hannah, loftily.

'Her plumes are her own; and her fan is her own, and her flowers will be her own in her own little pearl and silver holder; and Mama has given her a bracelet, small pearls on a chain of silver.'

'Fine feathers make fine birds,' said Hannah, roughly. 'But mere feathers don't count for much when it comes to the plucking.' But her hard face softened a little. 'Nevertheless...'

Nevertheless, she knocked that evening at the bedroom

door as Jane was dressing. 'I came to ask if you needed assistance. Payne was to have come but Arabella's hair will not satisfy either of them, and time is passing.' She added, with rare charity, that Arabella would probably have given up the struggle and sent her maid to Jane, but that Payne would not, for pride, let her young lady go out, not doing her hairdresser full justice. 'You, however, I see, have done yourself justice alone and unaided.'

She had propped Callie's picture against the looking-glass and worked to achieve the effect he had painted there. The pale hazel-brown hair very smooth and close; the single ringlet, released from a cluster of pearly-pink hot-house flowers and falling over one shoulder. She stood up with a rustle and swish of silken skirts. 'You are very kind. I thank you, ma'am, indeed. But I am finished; except that there do seem a great many tiny hooks and eyes.'

Miss Ferris pushed her, none too gently, to stand so that the light fell on the back of the bodice, and, with bent knees gradually straightening, fastened it upwards, ending with a large, strong concealed hook at the low oval of the neckline. 'Not well finished,' she said, examining the dress, fastidiously, 'but no doubt the dress-maker was rushed. And for the rest—for guesswork it fits not too badly.'

'I observed Miss Baines critically looking me over, that day at the shop. She must then have been assessing my measurements.'

'Oh, I dare say she's clever enough. A vulgar young creature, however, both in face and figure.'

'But not in spirit. What could exceed the delicacy of her feeling towards me?'

'Oh, most delicate indeed!—to be sending you garments, descending from heaven knew what source, and you ready to suppose that one or other of the gentlemen had come to your assistance.' But as Jane opened her mouth to disclaim (a trifle guiltily, however) Miss Ferris produced a flat box from her pocket. 'Well, I will be less intriguing in my bestowals. There! I am too old to wear it now; it's for a young girl—and if you must transform yourself from the sparrow into the peacock, we had better all do it thoroughly for you.'

A double row of seed pearls, all backed on to mother-of-pearl, small pearls stitched under the nacre to lift the whole up from the neck and prevent it from scratching. 'Miss Ferris—ma'am—I *could* not! I thank you with all my heart, but I could not!'

'Could not? You seem ready enough to take what others will offer you.'

'But this! This is—is of value,' said Jane, uncertainly.

'Nonsense, they're seed pearls and of no particular worth at all. And wear them you shall; unless of course you don't care for them?'

'*Care* for them!'

'My cousin would have given you a locket, but I prevented her. "She had better have my seed pearls," I said. "You have a thousand other trifles to choose from. Let me give her the necklace."'

'But—you disapprove of my going.'

'I disapprove of the governess going about as the family friend; and I believe you will find it uncomfortable to do so. For that matter, I disapprove of the family going to visit such people at all. But if you're to go, let us at least see you properly dressed. Now put it around your neck and let me do up the clasp; and no more nonsensical refusal or you will annoy me. And no more thanks, either,' said Cousin Hannah, fastening the pretty thing and standing back to look at Jane's reflection in the dressing-table mirror. 'There! That will do very well. Pick up your shawl and come along. You won't care, I suppose, for all your finery, to keep Lady Mellowes waiting?' Haughty, ungracious, she led the way out and down the stairs; but Jane followed her with a small, warm glow in her heart.

*   *   *

The Towers was a huge and complicated house, much built on to, both before and after the arrival of the Baines. 'I know it's not what it should be,' Mrs. Baines would say in her frank, jolly way—rather endearing to those who would but accept it, however repelling to those who would not. 'But we bought it before we understood proper ways and the fact of the matter is that I'm afraid we *like* it. And if we kept to our own ways I daresay it would be a lot less possible even than it now seems to be though I'm sure a great deal more comfortable. Poor Baines declares he can't sit a moment still on these bird-legged chairs and I'm sure if he breaks one a month he breaks half a dozen. However, when in Rome do as Rome does, or you'll not become Romans; and for Aurora's sake Baines and I must become Romans till we marry her off to some Caesar or whoever it was were the great gentlemen in those times. And even then, I suppose must continue to keep up appearances for our co-in-laws when they come about. With the dear Duke and Duchess!' Or the Marquis or the Earl, Mrs. Baines would amend, comfortably laughing. They by no means insisted upon the strawberries or nothing.

'Strawberry *leaves*, Mama,' Aurora would correct, also laughing. Aurora's sights, alas! were set considerably lower than Mama and Papa's. 'What should I do with all that hot ermine and horrid hard coronet?' It perhaps did not occur to Miss Baines that aristocratic ladies did not cling to these trappings by way of every day apparel.

The ballroom was enormous, built on for her début, though by now Mrs. Baines had become 'educated' and its style was impeccable. Perhaps a shade too over-chandelier'd the great ladies would confide (who, however, in considerable numbers, were happy enough to bring marriageable daughters to a house where one might meet all and sundry, but at least met *all*) and no expense had been spared to an extent that was almost indecent. But the champagne was of the highest quality throughout the evening; not just a glass of the best for the first few sips and then what would do very well when the palate was jaded; and the supper, laid out in the vast dining-room, not in some pitched-up tent in the grounds, with the draughts swirling round one's silk-stockinged ankles —was always superb and lavish. Aurora disappointed of a marquee such as all her grand friends had had, had upon this occasion, it was true, insisted that the dining-room be hung with striped canvas to look like a tent if she could not have one; but what matter for that? said the chaperones charitably, finding the draughts to be missing. (And who was the young lady accompanying the Dowager Lady Mellowes? Positively, she cut out that pert little Miss Arabella, and that took some doing!) They glanced a thought uneasily at this new possible rival to their own young aspirants.

Dominic had been at the foot of the vast sweep of marble steps to greet them and hand over the flowers, fresh but half an hour from the hot-houses. Adorabella in her pink, pale as a sea-shell, caught up with small garlands of green leaves and silk roses, bubbled with anticipation and sweet temper; the pink, worn with some daring in contrast to the auburn hair, in fact set it off to perfection. Dominic's eyes stared down into the happily smiling little face with a dog-like devotion. The Dowager, still almost as pretty as her daughter, descended from the carriage in her apricot silk ornamented with a heavy, creamy-coloured Irish lace. And after her—Miss Jane Bird.

Miss Jane Bird—Miss Shining Dove in a swirl of dove-blue, dove-green silk, with pearls about her slender throat and the long, soft hazel curl falling from the smooth head to a round white shoulder. Dominic, stepping forward to hand the bouquet of flowers in its filagree'd holder, stopped absolutely dumb-struck. Callie, seeing Arabella open-eyed looking on, nudged him sharply, took the flowers and with a bow handed them to the lady. 'You are my picture come to life,' he said in a voice that shook a little. 'I am proved at last to be a very great artist!'

'I think our dove looks most lovely,' said Lady Mellowes, with a half-uneasy glance at her daughter.

'So do I,' said Adorabella, pulling herself together, generous in praise. 'Truly lovely.' She took her cousin's arm and went on up the steps with him.

Callie followed with Jane. 'Oh, dear! Are you not in danger of becoming just a little *too* lovely?'

'I have never been so in my life before,' she said simply. 'Just for my one brief hour—let me enjoy it!'

He turned to look at her, smiling. 'Yes, enjoy it! Drink your fill of it. These hours don't last long in our butterfly days; we must keep such brief moments of perfection while we can.' And he said, with his own old mockery: 'For me the perfection already has departed: for who now will plan a match for you with the poor old ex-tutor?' But at her anxious glance, he laughed, pressing her arm for a moment close against his own. 'Don't let even a moment of alarm spoil your hour. That dream was a dream never dreamed: I give you my word on it. You are and ever shall be my dear friend, Miss Dove, the little governess; the beautiful lady is for me confined ever in a picture.'

The long line awaiting presentation to the host and hostess and Miss Aurora. The curious glances, the whispers. All eyes on Adorabella, accepted belle of the neighbourhood; but sweeping on to the young lady with the smooth head carried so swanlike on the perfect throat and neck, in the dress with its swirl of iridescent silk. A hundred voices questioning: 'Who *is* she?'

And Dorabella, turning her head to whisper, close and confiding: 'Have you seen him? Where is he?'

He was there. Standing talking, negligently leaning back against a pillar, champagne glass in hand ... The tall figure, the fair head, the face bent down over an upturned, lovely young face: the blue eyes smiling down, dancing down in that look that said, 'I find you enchanting, I find you adorable...'

Mr. Richard Havering: in conversation with the Honourable Clarissa Somebody—or would it be 'the Rutherford girl'? Mrs. Edgar Worcester it was unlikely to be; with or without her husband from Mayfair. And the lady from Capsicum Street—well, hardly! But Mr. Richard Havering looked down into her eyes, and her eyes smiled back at him in happy acceptance of conquest.

Lady Mellowes went quietly by. Adorabella looked steadily ahead and, her hand hooked lightly into her cousin's arm, went quietly by. Miss Jane Bird bit on her lip—and went quietly by.

He glanced up; saw her. Under his breath he said: 'Dear God!'

His partner was pardonably startled. 'What do you say?'

'I beg your pardon! Did I say something? I caught my hand on a roughness of the pillar here.' He sucked on the edge of his palm with an expression of somewhat over-done agony. 'If I may return you to your chaperone, per-haps I should retire for a moment and take out the splinter.'

The splinter did not take long; a very short while later found him bowing before Lady Mellowes' chair. 'Your ladyship looks all that is lovely tonight; and as for these two flowers you bring in your bouquet—or should I say this pair of doves...!'

'We have just passed you, cooing to a very pretty pigeon of your own,' said Dorabella, coolly.

'No pigeon of mine. The lady is engaged to the fortunate Sir Edward Lasalle.'

'I will stand your second,' promised Callie, coming as ever to the rescue, 'when, as doubtless is imminent, Sir Edward challenges you to pistols at dawn.'

'I could hardly stand silent; I must do my duty by my hostess—and, till perfection arrives, make do with second best.' He sketched a little bow to both the young ladies, but it was to Adorabella that he addressed himself, avoiding Jane's eye. 'You will not have forgotten our wager? I claim the first dance.'

The light came back to the lovely little face, the almost childishly innocent face that lit up so readily to a return of happiness. 'Yes, you won. And you see the result before you!'

'Our dove is indeed a radiant dove tonight.' But still he avoided the direct look, concentrating upon the tiny programme, complete with pencil, hanging from Jane's gloved wrist. 'May I put myself down for a waltz? The first is commanded already—I dance it with my hostess. But the first after supper?'

'Oh, Rich—oh, Mr. Havering, you always waltz with *me*!'

'The last with you then, Miss Mellowes, if I may be so bold as to claim two dances. Lady Mellowes will permit me? The first, then?—and the last waltz?'

'And the gallop at the end?'

'Arabella,' said Lady Mellowes, sharply. 'You forget yourself. You behave like a child.' To Mr. Havering she said, but quietly: 'Two dances will be enough. You will get yourselves talked about.'

'To be talked about in conjunction with Miss Mellowes,' he said, shifting the blue look towards her mother, 'would be more happiness than any man could endure and live. For my safety's sake therefore—' and he looked back to Adorabella, laughing, '—we had better confine it to two dances. When the music strikes up, then, I shall find you here? Till then I must make way for other admirers.' He walked off, gaily smiling.

Lady Mellowes looked after him. 'Really that young man is ... Well, it must be confessed that he has a disarming way with him.' But she turned anxious eyes towards her daughter. 'My dearest—he is light of heart. Do beware!' she said.

Dominic had taken Dorabella's card, filled in, as though

of right, a couple of dances. 'Miss Dove—may I beg the first with you?'

'Oh, thank you,' she said, grateful to be assured of one at least. 'I shall be so delighted.'

'You mustn't thank gentlemen for wishing to dance with you,' said Adorabella, laughing. 'It's they who should be on their knees, to implore you. Just graciously permit them.'

'I did not observe you a moment ago, just graciously permitting Mr. Havering,' said Dominic, not smiling.

She was taken aback. 'Oh—well—it's only that he's such a good dancer!'

'He's making very sure that his talents won't be wasted,' said Lady Mellowes, with, in her, a most unusual asperity. 'Aurora Baines is all happiness, he has been scribbling earnestly in Lady Caroline Leslie's programme; now we see him making his way over to little Miss Feather.' Lady Caroline had recently inherited from her grandmother, she added casually; and Miss Feather, of course ... 'But I fear he wastes his time there. Mr. Feather is one of Mr. Baines' cronies and I think did not amass all he has for the benefit of a prodigal son-in-law.'

'Mama, you insult him! Because a young woman has some fortune—'

'I say only that he has a rare gift for finding out only the young women with fortunes.'

'There are none other here. Where, in this room, shall he find any girl with no money?'

'I am a girl with no money,' said Jane, seconding her. 'And he has found me. He asks me for two dances: not one, as I daresay he might feel obliged to—but two. No one can pretend that that is for my fortune.'

But a gentleman had appeared, was kissing Lady Mellowes' gloved fingers, kissing Dorabella's. 'If I might crave a dance with the adorable Mees Mellowes ... ?'

'But of course, Count. I'm sure my daughter will be happy ...'

98

Dorabella looked not markedly happy but was obliged to accept. The Count turned regretful eyes upon Miss Bird, was desolated that for the rest his programme was full. 'He doesn't yet know who she is; must discover first for certain that she is worth his trouble. Now there, Mama,' said Dorabella, resentfully, 'is a real fortune hunter. Yet I must dance with *him*.'

'I thought you would be happy to,' said Lady Mellowes, coolly teasing. 'He is a very good dancer—which you give as your only reason for wishing to accept certain other gentlemen.'

A Mr. Foster succeeded him; scribbled in both young ladies' programmes, made way for others. 'You see—you are a success,' said Adorabella, whispering. 'Your programme is half full already.'

'They come first to ask *you*; the crumbs fall to me from your table. But don't think I complain,' Jane assured her, laughing. 'The hungry man is only too glad of the sustenance.'

Aurora, released from her duties in the receiving line, came bustling by, very plain in her unbecoming white dress, but all smiles and friendship. 'I cannot help saying myself that the dress is perfect,' she said, sitting down for a moment beside Jane. 'You look truly beautiful. Everyone is admiring you. Several gentlemen already have asked who you are. I just say,' she added, in a momentary embarrassment, 'that you are in Lady Mellowes' party.'

'I shall tell them all in what capacity,' said Jane. 'I don't want any pretences.' It would be—profitable, if no more pleasing than that, she thought, to study their reactions. Friend or foe? she would in essence be saying. Would Callie think her 'missish' and perhaps ill-mannered? She supposed that he would; but the fierce underlying pride insisted within herself: 'I'll sail under no false colours.'

The dance with Dominic was a pleasure, though she felt a little uneasy in the warmth of his attentions. Across the room, she looked out for Dorabella, fearing an attack of jealousy; but Dorabella was dancing in the arms of Richard Havering and had eyes for no others. Dominic apparently was also watching them. 'Dorabella is right. Havering's a good dancer.'

'I hope so; since I am destined to waltz with him.'

'He'll be better at it than I, that's one thing certain. I'm afraid I'm not a ladies' man as they call it. I love my home and the place, the stables and the dogs, all the people ... To run a great estate—that's not to be just some homespun clod of a farmer. There's interest and intelligence in maintaining a fine stable, stocking the river with trout—you should come one day and let me show you the stews where we raise the fingerlings, grading their feeding and conditions, bringing them gradually to be fine stout fish, capable of finding their way in their own element.'

'Which, left to themselves, you despair of their doing?'

'You laugh; but you'd find they'd not be so fat and fine, and the majority would have perished long before they came to maturity.'

'And so to your hook. It's like bringing back the prisoner to health before you hang him. A hearty breakfast.'

'The fish takes his chance,' said Dominic. 'He shouldn't be so greedy after flies.' But he looked down at her, his handsome young face full of appreciative laughter. 'You are teasing me!'

'Not at all. I accept all you say. I know in fact that you put great thought and study into the care of your farms and the land that goes with them.'

'Well—we do: I and my men. I won't claim all the glory for myself, they are splendid people. But they don't come to such places as this—and I think are none the worse off for it. I like a good dinner as well as the next man—good talk and plenty of laughter, and afterwards some music in the drawing-room—'

'Adorabella, and her delicious little voice singing?'

'She or another; though it's true that not all young ladies are aware of the limits of their ability. It's not always unadulterated pleasure. But ... Well, that I find all comfortable and civilised. Who can hold a conversation, hopping about like this?—constantly parted and brought together, only again to be parted...'

'You and I are not doing too badly; we've never before conversed like this together.'

'We've never before *been* together; not by ourselves—we have always been two of a party.' They divided again in the dance; when they met he had evidently been thinking. He said rather wistfully: 'Shouldn't you, as a woman, like to be mistress of such an estate as we've been discussing?'

'Very much,' she said, and asked, teasing again: 'Are you making me an offer?'

'Alas,' he said, pretending regret, 'that my poor heart is already bespoken.'

'And by one who, however little she may outwardly value it, does not care to see it at the mercy of any other young lady.' She said, more earnestly: 'Do you think you are entirely wise in your—game—of trying to make Adorabella jealous?'

'You are a too perceptive young lady, Miss Bird,' he said.

'Just as well, perhaps—suppose I also had been deceived.' But she smiled at him. 'Have no fear; I am quite proof against such a misconception as that might be!'

Her hand in the crook of his elbow, they walked out on to the terrace. Several couples already were there, taking in a breath of the warm spring evening air, before the young ladies rejoined their chaperones. Adorabella was standing at the balustrade with her partner. Her face was lovely in its ecstasy of happiness and, glancing, Jane saw that the small hand crept towards his till their fingers were touching. 'What a fool I am,' she thought, 'that I should suppose that it will mean anything to him to hold me in his arms and dance with me!' Half a dozen other girls at that moment perhaps were thinking of their coming moments with Richard Havering. He is light of heart, Lady Mellowes had said: do beware! Had her remark been addressed only to her daughter?

Back in her place at Lady Mellowes' side, she found a gentleman bowing over her hand, a tall, handsome man, easy mannered, well dressed. 'Our dance, Miss Bird? I believe it is to be my happiness...?'

She glanced at her programme. Mr. Edward Foster. As, in a sort of dream, she floated away on his arm, she said to him: 'I am so glad that you should be plain Mr. Foster.'

'So am I, since it means that I answer to the name on your programme. But may I ask why your preference should be for a plain gentleman?—which my looking glass tells me is but too true; though a young lady has never before been so frank with me.'

'You're making fun of me,' she said. 'You know I didn't mean it that way.'

'What way, then?' He handed her, bowing, into their place in the set. She curtsied back, low. 'Only that ... If I tell you, you will—you won't think well of me. But you are the first I've spoken to; and I've made up my mind to tell everyone.'

'You don't single me out for exclusion as to this wonderful confidence; but at least I am honoured by priority.'

'And yet that is only an accident, too,' she said, laughing. 'For—except for Mr. Mellowes, who knows of it—you're the first on my programme.'

'No accident, I assure you. I cut my way through a great mob to secure the place...'

All so easy; so dream like and easy, easy flow of idle repartee, idle flirtation, un-fraught with the smallest danger. The dance parted them; they met again, touched hands, again parted. When at last they stood together once more, he insisted: 'And what now of the revelation too long postponed...? You're going to tell me that you are a mermaid come up from the sea in your sea-green dress: that you'll vanish at midnight.'

'You're not so far off,' she said. 'I am indeed a Cinderella.'

'Plain Mr. Foster will appear first thing in the morning to try the glass slipper.'

'You won't have far to look. You will find me at Lady Mellowes', at the Dower House. I am Miss Arabella's paid companion.'

She felt his arm stiffen and for a moment her heart sank. But he relaxed at once. 'Miss Mellowes is fortunate...' But he broke off. 'Let us for a moment abandon persiflage. Why do you so carefully hand me this piece of information?'

'I have what I think is a natural fear, of sailing under false colours.'

He turned down upon her a look of great kindness. 'Well, but how sweet!' he said. 'What an honest courage! What a remarkable young lady!'

She said rather wistfully: 'Then you don't object to dance with me?'

He raised her hand and laid a brief kiss upon her fingers. 'Do you know,' he said, 'you so touch my heart that at this moment I think there is no young lady in all this room that I would less object to dance with.'

Nor with her next partner was she any less fortunate. He was a big, rather bucolic young man, squire of a small but excellent estate on the other side of the county. 'I know your name, Miss Bird, and that you are apparently a friend of my Adorabella.' He grinned, a little rueful grimace. 'Adorabella to me,' he amended. 'That she is mine, alas is not true; though not for want of asking.'

'I fear that that applies to only too many broken hearts here tonight.'

'Hearts mend,' he said, shrugging again. 'At least we must pray that they do; otherwise these parts are like to be populated in thirty years time, with nothing but crusty old bachelors. And one other thing I must tell you before I ask questions of my own: though this you may I fear have discovered for yourself already. I am a very bad dancer.'

'You prefer a dining-room to a ballroom,' suggested Jane, 'and no place to your estate and your stables and kennels and stew-ponds; and think a glass of port and a little music in the drawing-room, more worth having than any amount of this hopping about and meeting only to part again...' She laughed up at his puzzled face. 'It's my fate to dance tonight only with gentlemen who would frankly prefer to be at home having a good dinner.'

'No one could continue so, who found himself with a partner of so much wit and beauty.'

'Your gallantry matches your dancing, sir; and for my part I find no fault with either.'

'I come back to my original question,' he said. 'You are a friend of Miss Mellowes? May I know more of you?'

'Yes, I'm very happy to tell you; I intended to do so, I prefer to tell everyone. I am Miss Mellowes' paid governess and companion.'

Again the tiny stiffening of surprise—and shock? But he had not quite the smoothness to gloss over it, as had Mr. Foster. He pulled back and away, to look down into her face. 'Are you in*deed*? You amaze me!'

'And somewhat shock you?'

'I had thought a governess an elderly lady wearing worsted mittens over poor chalky fingers...'

'You see me in disguise. I am playing Cinderella.'

'Fairy god-mothers must be working over-hours,' he said, simply...

And Lord George Chalmers. Lord George Chalmers really *was* the son of a Duchess. 'That wicked looking old woman sitting over there beside Lady Mellowes. She looks wicked and old because she is both. But she is my mother.'

'I wonder if she knows that her son is dancing with Lady Mellowes' daughter's governess?'

'Are you a governess indeed?' he said, without any check. 'You don't look like one. And as to my mother, she would be perfectly delighted. She seeks everywhere for just such a stern young lady as a governess must be, to take me in hand. I'm addicted to terrible vices and she despairs of me. And *for* me. No other young woman will look twice at me—or be allowed to by her mama, if she would? But for a governess to attach a peer of the realm—how could she resist it? Shall we not go over immediately and break the glad news to Mama?'

'You must at least first allow me breath to say "But this is so sudden!"''

'Well, it may be a little precipitate. We will wait till the next ball. By then, however, I shall expect you to have considered my proposition carefully and be ready with an answer.'

'Oh, but certainly!' she said. 'I'll think over all the pros and cons. You have been so explicit!' She parted from him and returned to Lady Mellowes. 'I have had my first proposal,' she said. 'And from a Marquis.'

'His mother's just been speaking of him. She longs to find a nice, steady girl for him.'

'He's found one for himself. He assures me I shall suit him perfectly. Whether he will equally suit me,' said Jane, laughing, 'is another question. He's just a little over-whelming.'

Lady Mellowes looked back, smiling, into the glowing face. 'And you also are a little over-whelming this evening,' she said, almost tenderly. 'Our dove has spread its shining wings and soars like a bird of paradise.'

'*In* paradise,' said Jane, smiling back at her. 'If only for this lovely hour; if only for this fleeting moment.' (For was not heaven approaching?—the blue heaven of her whole heart's longing. 'In a little while,' she thought, 'I shall be dancing in his arms...!)

Her next partner failed to appear; instead there came a message, he had suffered a small accident, wrenched an ankle, must with infinite regret beg to be excused their engagement. She was not sorry for the rest; only a little discomfited to feel that people might observe her as a wallflower, partnerless. Lady Mellowes said, rising: 'Well, as it's the supper dance, my dear, we may as well go through. Dorabella's partner will look after *her*.' Several ladies, similarly relieved of their charges, came to join her. 'We will all make up a table together; it will be delicious...'

But hardly for a young lady in a shimmering ball gown —nodding heads with aunts and mamas, Mrs. Somebody's hopes for dear Amelia with her charming young Sir Thomas, Lady So-and-so's bewailing at dear Charles's insistence upon marrying that Halford gal, a sweet gal, my dear, but *not* what his father and I had planned for him ... Shall I feign headache, she thought?—ask for permission to be allowed to go to the ladies' resting room for a little while. But...

But a gentleman was approaching across the ballroom floor—a very small, slender man, limping on a cane, a slight but apparent malformation of the left foot. A beautiful cane: amber, delicately carved. But everything about him, in fact, was exquisitely appointed. His hair was impeccably groomed, his handsome face very smooth as though he had that moment emerged from his barber's hands; his linen marvellously got up, his dress almost dandified, though not disagreeably so, and exactly becoming him. Very difficult to gauge his age: near to middle age, certainly, the face unlined and yet marked with the experience of suffering—a something perhaps in the light blue eyes, in the set of the mouth ... He bowed over Lady Mellowes' hand. 'I hope your ladyship has not forgotten our earlier meeting; at the Duchess of Graham's, I think?—a delightful encounter, for me at any rate.'

'But of course I've not forgotten,' said Lady Mellowes, and about her the chaperones coo'ed: who would forget an encounter with Sir Frederick Travenne?—and how could that ever have been less than delightful? It was apparent that Sir Frederick, for all his lack of inches, was a favourite at least with the older ladies.

'I remember it very well, Sir Frederick; and your promise to show me one day over Robin's Grange; we all know that it's a very miracle of beauty.'

He bowed. 'An agreeable house, Madam; and it's true that I flatter myself on being something of a connoisseur of beautiful things.' He glanced down with a sort of self-deprecation, at his halting left foot. 'Having little other form of occupation possible to me, I amuse myself by collecting them.' He addressed himself to Lady Mellowes, but his look had turned towards Jane. 'In fact it is as a connoisseur and collector, that I apply to you now. I observed from across the room that your lovely companion is not engaged for this dance. I hadn't dared to approach her earlier, being only too apparently, not myself a performer; but if I might beg her now to allow me to take her in to supper—?'

'Yes, indeed, Sir Frederick, I'm sure Miss Bird will be too happy.' Lady Mellowes performed brief introductions. 'Miss Bird was disappointed of the partner to whom she was engaged; he was unfortunately prevented.'

'Unfortunately for *him*,' said Sir Frederick. 'His loss is all to my advantage.' He stood back while the ladies, nodding and beaming, sailed on to the refreshment room. 'Shall we stay back a moment and let them settle before we find our own niche?' And he bowed and smiled to her. 'You don't object, Miss Bird, to this stealing away of you from your moment of solitude?'

'No indeed. Any young lady's moment of such solitude is spent in prayer that none will suppose it to be for any lack of alternative. Did you not observe my look of haughty repudiation?—to make sure that all would recognise that I went in to supper with my elders by choice, not because I was among the unchosen.'

They were moving now towards the supper room; he leaning on his stick, not offering her his arm. 'If you seriously imagine that anyone could suppose such a thing, you must indeed by very thin-skinned, Miss Bird.'

'Well—I am perhaps. Indeed, I am in a fair way to being thin-skinned,' she said. 'I am a paid governess.'

No check here. He said calmly: 'You tell me so because you're afraid that I shall assume something grander—and be disappointed?'

'Or affronted: at my temerity in intruding into this company.'

The ballroom was half deserted, a few couples swooned round, making their way as they danced towards the exits; the chaperones swept by in small, self-sufficient groups, silks swishing, heads, elaborately dressed with embellishments of feather and bows, nid-nodding together. He stopped, facing her; no taller than herself, a slender, slip of a man, his eyes on the same level looking directly into hers. 'Poor girl!' he said. 'How deep you must suffer that you should grasp this nettle so firmly and hand it out, I suppose, to all who approach you!' He glanced down at his foot. 'I speak as one also familiar with an irrational humility.'

'Because you are a little lame—that's no cause to be ashamed; that's not your own doing.'

'I daresay it's not your own doing that you find yourself in a situation so unworthy. Unworthy, I mean, of so lovely a creature with so delicate a spirit. You were born for better things than to crush down all this beauty and brightness into the mould of a dependent.'

He had begun to move forward again. She said quickly: 'It's an easy dependency. All is kindness and goodness—don't think I have anything to complain of there. As you see me now—everything is due to their bounty. Am I mean of spirit, therefore, still to be resentful of my lot?'

'If you are,' he said, 'then what better am I? I have so much to compensate me. And yet ... I see the girls turn away, hoping that I shan't make them look ridiculous by forcing them to dance with a limping dwarf; *you* fancy, I suppose, that your partners will feel their pride in some way undermined: as though they had been caught kissing the housemaid.' He smiled at her with great kindness. 'Though the housemaid be the prettiest girl in all the land.'

They found the niche he had promised. 'I have plenty of time while others are dancing to make these small reconnaissances,' he said, laughing. 'I like things just my way.' His way was usually to single out the more charming of the chaperones and beg two or three to join him in his little private arena of elegance and calm. 'They all dote upon me. I have my small compensations, after all. They long, of course, for me to place The Grange at the feet of one or other of their more ineligible daughters, the ones they're beginning to despair of ever getting settled. If my famed ill-health should then leave the young lady rapidly widowed, of course all would be perfection...' He waved a small, elegant hand to a passing waiter. 'You will not have forgotten my just exactly chilled champagne...?'

Aurora's fancy had not stopped at a tent built within the great dining hall; the whole must be imbued with the air of a picnic, the lanterns hanging, wreathed in ivy, walls festooned with evergreens, great swathes of country flowers and grasses snaking down the long tables, groaning with picnic food. Was there ever such a picnic?—iced soups, fish and fowl, broken down, deliciously confected, and rebuilt into their own shapes, painted with scales or feathers to a fantastic semblance of reality. Boars' heads the same, glazed and shining richly brown, with great protruding tusks of fresh *foie gras*; bowls of salad fragrant with herbs, a hundred different shapes and jellies, great mounds of creamy cakes and confections, glasses of syllabub, little sweetmeats of marzipan, chocolate, ginger, iced and decorated; great, fat, juicy crystallised fruits, tiny *bonne bouches* of violets and rose petals dipped in honey ... Nothing but what one might get at a picnic, Aurora insisted! And champagne, champagne, and champagne, flowing so that never a glass was more than sipped at but it was filled to the brim again ... 'Quantity is not a characteristic one necessarily respects,' said Sir Frederick, toying with fruit and wine, 'but when it goes hand in hand with such quality as this, really one must take off one's hat and say, Hurrah for Papa and Mama Baines! —and for Miss Aurora whose behests they so handsomely obey...'

'You won't let me drink just one sip more of this delicious wine?'

'No, I won't have it said that I couldn't keep a lovely young lady by my side unless I first rendered her tipsy. Come let's creep out of this convenient french window and, in the evening air, undo the effects of all this food and drink...'

They walked there a long time, he limping on his carved amber cane, she with one hand slipped lightly into his free arm. He dropped his light manner, a little affected, a little over-polished and *à la mode*; talked to her of his home and of his treasures, of the travels that had collected them together. 'I have a new painting which is at the moment my especial joy; a Madonna from Italy, I'm convinced that she's by Bellini. I'm consulting Mr. Richard Havering about her—you know him, of course? He is a considerable expert and knows something of cleaning and restoring—I hope he will help me.' If he noticed the slight tremor of her hand at that name, he did not show it; but he shifted the conversation from his own life and to hers. She told him of the happy days succeeded by the long domination by the grim, narrow, bigoted old aunt. 'No escape for the dove, then, from that cage of despair?'

'No escape. How could I go? I owed her so much that

had been expended on my poor mother. Stone walls do not a prison make,' said Jane, 'but many a prison, I think, is built from necessary gratitude; from an obligation to repay. How could the poor dove fly over such walls as those? Its wings were clipped.'

'And so remain—though for other reasons and, I hope, in less onerous confinement. Nevertheless...'

Nevertheless...

He was quiet for what seemed a long time: musing. He said at last: 'If I say something—you will not misunderstand me...? You won't be offended if I speak to you a little from my heart? It is only this.' He was silent again. 'My sister lives with me—she is older than I and widowed and I hope she will live with me always. Therefore, I make bold to say this: if ever you are in need—homeless, helpless, at the mercy of a world too hard for you—keep close this promise that I make to you now. We have little in common but our poor, too-easily wounded pride; but however things may change, in however distant a future—if you will turn to me—to us—whenever you may be in need—neither I nor my sister will ever fail you...' His head had been bent over the glossy amber knob of the cane; now at her silence, he looked up sharply, saw that her mind had wandered from his words and said at once in a new, light tone: 'You're in need of refreshment. A water-ice?' and leaning on the cane, limped away immediately, leaving her there alone.

She had been conscious over his words of a voice heard only as a murmur on the far side of a wall dividing the terrace from a bayed-out window of the ballroom. Now, cutting across the silence that followed his departure, she caught one word too familiar to remain unrecognised. A voice was saying: 'A *governess*?'

'Governess to Lady Mellowes' daughter. No money there, alas, my dear fellow! Not a penny.'

That voice! The voice that had said, 'Our dove is a

radiant dove tonight.' No money, my dear fellow, not a penny!

Another voice, a third voice, saying something she could not catch. And Richard Havering answering, 'I think, my lord, you'd find the young lady, whatever she may appear on the outside, not very—amiable.'

Sir Frederick had intercepted a waiter and returned with water-ices, orange and lemon. They entered upon a light wrangle as to who should have orange, who lemon. But she had little heart for badinage. The magic was gone. He sensed it; perhaps was offended—she could not care. He suggested: 'The music will be starting again. I must return you to your chaperone,' and, not offering his arm, occupied as he must be by his own effort to make progress with dignity aided by the carved amber cane, turned— and she must follow. But in any event, by now the voices in the ballroom window were to be heard no more.

She went with him, listlessly; curtsied her thanks, sat down on the little gilt chair beside her ladyship. 'No money there, my dear fellow! Not a penny.' And some lordship would find the young lady not very amiable ...

And the next dance on the programme was her waltz with him.

One hand behind her waist, supporting her, one hand holding her hand, close and firm; blue eyes looking down at her, a swirl about her of wafting taffetas—dancing. He had spoken not a word, simply come to her, bowed, held out his hand, guided her on to the dance floor. Now he said: 'It's just as it had to be. How should a dove dance but like a little bird?—lightly as though on the wing; beneath the coloured plumage almost nothing in one's arms.'

She tried to reply, but could not: she who had so light-heartedly chattered with her other partners. About them, the dancing couples moved and spun in a maze of blurred colour, the lights glittered down in a brilliance that seemed suddenly hard and searching. He said, surprised: 'You are very silent?'

Her heart was sick with the pain of it, the bewilderment; the bitter disappointment that here in this moment that was to have been her one little glimpse of heaven, all was now spoilt and sour. She said almost sullenly: 'There seems nothing very much to speak of.'

'We will speak of you. Of how lovely you look, of how everyone present is admiring you.'

'Oh, yes,' she said bitterly. 'I've heard something of their expressions of admiration. And of how those were received by their hearers.'

'Has someone distressed you?' And he gathered her a little closer, and the gleam was a gleam no longer but a soft ray, gently probing into her heart's soreness: 'Has that quiet pride of yours been somehow offended? Because of your—situation...?'

'No, indeed,' she said. 'I tell everyone frankly what is my—situation, as you call it; and everyone I've told has been kind and accepted it and accepted me into their kindness; even though I be simply Lady Mellowes' governess and without a penny.' She did not dare add, 'nor any amiability either'. It would be too mortifying if he should guess that she had heard in what terms he had spoken of her.

'Then I can only be sorry that you should seem so unhappy.'

'I am perfectly happy. In my borrowed plumes, with all the young ladies in the room at this moment so jealously watching me—I can hardly fail to be happy.'

'They're jealous of your loveliness,' he said. 'How could they not be?'

'Beauty is skin deep. In my case, the depth of my borrowed plumage.'

'This is not for you to judge,' he said, skilfully steering her, skimming over the surface of the polished floor with ease so practised that he need give it no attention.

'One can but be thankful for so great a mercy,' he said, smiling down at her. 'To think that in the course of an hour's entertainment, we might have lost you for ever!'

'Little danger of that,' she said, 'where all the gentlemen present are intent only upon the wealth of the various prospects.'

Again the slight check; but she seemed to have disarmed his suspicion though, unable in her bitterness to stop herself, she played with fire. He said, still smiling: 'That is hardly for Miss Dove to declare; who has found at least two gentlemen—three, if I may dare to include myself among the devotees—less mercenarily inclined.'

'I hardly regard myself as a prospect,' she said, coldly. 'And just as well!—since we have included amiability as a pre-requisite. Someone, no doubt will be found to disillusion my admirers on that point before they come to renew their importunings.'

He looked down at her curiously; slowed down the pacing of their dancing almost to a stillness: 'What has happened to Miss Dove, who should be all gentle docility, so to sharpen her little beak to hardness?' She did not answer. He broke out abruptly, almost bursting out with it, accelerating their pace again to a giddy whirligig: 'I don't care for this dress! It's so much admired—but for myself, I don't care for it.'

'Nor I for your opinion, sir. I did not invite it.'

'Miss *Dove!*' he exclaimed: almost shocked. She knew that her face had gone pale and now saw that his also had lost colour, and thought wretchedly that all her lovely world was tumbling to pieces, that she should have been shaken into speaking so harshly to him, so roughly and crudely, losing for ever the hope that would not die in her breast, of ever seeing again that gleam of blue that turned her poor heart to water. 'I beg your pardon. I didn't mean to speak so sharply. But everyone has been praising my dress; it was so kindly given—'

'And has brought you to the ball,' he said, more quietly.

'So we should all be grateful to it. But I say only that, charming as it is and well as of course it becomes you, it's not what *I* should have chosen for you. It's too full of colour, too much of a—of a dress with a pretty young lady inside it, instead of a pretty young lady wearing a dress. It seems to—to take hold of you.' She knew that he meant that in the dress she was not the person he knew; not she who had been the recipient of that gleam. But he continued only: '*I* would dress you in far gentler colours than this, in pale corals and gold, to set off this clear, pale skin; in tones of russet and silver ... I love you best in your own soft browns and greys, your doves and sepias, with their delicate sheen.'

And the music ended; and he led her without another word, out of the dance and towards the place where Adorabella and Lady Mellowes awaited her.

She went through the rest of the evening in a dream: hardly knew that she danced again and yet again, nor whether she troubled to warn all and sundry that she was but a governess, had not a penny, was not even to be trusted to make herself—amiable. As the last dance approached, she said to Lady Mellowes, almost desperately: 'I'm tired and jaded. May I go to the rest room until the ball is over? If Mr. Havering comes for his polka —would you please ask him to excuse me; say that I'm indisposed ... ?'

Lady Mellowes' governess ... Not a penny, my dear fellow ... Your lordship would find the young lady not very—amiable ...

But ...

But: *I love you best in your own soft browns and greys.*

'He cannot resist the conquest of a woman; that is all it is,' she said in her weary heart.

Chapter 7

Both young ladies, by her ladyship's permission, rose late next morning—meeting in the converted schoolroom, Dorabella all sparkle and reminiscence, Jane heavy-eyed and inattentive. 'How could you have foregone the last dance with him? He was like a lost soul—he, whom every girl in the room most longed to dance with—without a partner...'

'Surely some young lady somehow made herself—accidentally—available?'

'Yes, and who do you think it was?—that depressing little Feathers girl, whose partner would have been Tom Hoyle, the man who hurt his ankle and couldn't dance with you, you recall? So she was available and willy nilly he must dance with her and that made it *three times*! And he doesn't care for her, not at all really, so that shows he's not interested, as they all say he is, only in wealth; for she's rich as Croesus...'

'Well, and that brings us, Dorabella, to our reading of ancient history. Who was Croesus?'

'Oh, for heaven's sake, you wouldn't plague me with that stuff on the day after a ball? He was a rich old man and wouldn't listen to some other old man called Solon, or the other way about, though I think it's the first, for everybody listens to rich old men. Even you, Miss Dove. I saw you positively rapt in conversation with that handsome Mr. Foster.'

'Mr. Foster, as I recall him, must be something under thirty.'

'Thirty if a day. Not yet a wooden leg, I grant you. And speaking of wooden legs, how did you fare with Sir Frederick Whatsisname? Isn't he the dandiest, daintiest little fellow? All the mamas adore him, and the girls too, though it's such a waste to spend time with him since he's a hundred years old and of course doesn't dance. His house is a museum of possessions, everything he has is perfect, they say his very horse is a pure bred Arabian, son or grandson or some such relative of that famous Mr. Darley's.'

'Mr. Darley has been dead these hundred years and a great deal more; and doubtless his horse also.'

'Well, well, in a direct line; how nippitty you are this morning!' Nippitty was a great word of Adorabella's for any failure in loving kindness and total agreement with everything she said. 'Now, come, tell me every word! You danced with Him—what did you talk about, did he say anything of *me*?'

'If you mean Mr. Havering, I fear he made no mention of you.'

'Ah, well, I daresay he saved it all to say directly to me. Oh, the ecstasy of it! Does he not dance like an angel? And out on the terrace, he took my hand in his—'

'You offered him your hand, Dorabella, I saw you; and I think that was not quite a ladylike thing to do.'

'He took it, just the same, and held it in his and said that I looked lovely, I looked like my name...'

'Well, for that matter, he said much the same to me. Only my name—the name he used—is that of a dove, a grey, drab little bird.'

'Not all doves are grey. Your dress was in the colour of a different member of the species.'

'As to the dress, that was the other thing he said: he did not care for the dress.'

'Well! But how unkind! And not like him. He pays

compliments to everyone—I think that if a girl is plain, he the more compliments her, to make her feel sure of herself and happy. Miss Frere told me that he said her hands were like little white mushrooms: which is true, she has small, plump white hands—the only charming thing about her.'

'Except for her fortune?'

'Oh, I listen to none of that *canard*; he thinks nothing of money. He never even speaks of it.'

'Not to you; nor to Miss Frere nor Miss Baines nor to all the other Misses; not to me,' said Jane, bitterly. 'But he speaks of it.'

Adorabella opened huge deep blue eyes. 'Why, Miss Dove—don't you like him?'

'I don't trust him,' said Jane. 'That's all. Come, Dorabella, now, seriously—to our reading!'

Callie came to the Dower House, strolling down the hill to hear all about their pleasures at the ball. He had, in his own thoughtful way, refrained from asking either of them for a dance. Having satisfied himself that Miss Dove's programme was filled (there could never be any doubt as to Adorabella's) he had slipped away; there were too many others, he said, as ever without bitterness, for them to waste their time upon everyday familiar old Callie; they would form a four with Dominic one day and hop about in the hall at the Dower House and have a splendid time. And he had spent the rest of his evening with less favoured young women; to their infinite gratitude in many cases, where they sat with their chaperones, glued to the wall, grey with mortification at yet another repetition of their all too customary plight. 'Oh, Callie, you must be the best-hearted person in all the world!'

'Because *your* pretty head is too much filled with fun and flattery to be concerned with others, my dear Dorabella, doesn't mean they don't exist. And suffer. Besides,' said Callie, disclaiming too much virtue, 'it wasn't *all*, what I have heard you—spoilt little creature as you are—describe as "going slumming". I confess that where there was a pretty one free, I soon gobbled her up.' And anyway, he said, many of the plain girls were the better company. 'They're grateful, which makes them love you and that's always pleasant; and work hard to amuse, instead of supposing that the turn of a head here, the brush of a curl there will be sufficient entertainment for a man of intelligence. And they take you at face value and so don't grow stiff and resentful, supposing you only to be running after their riches. That little Miss Frere is a charmer—'

'And has hands like little mushrooms,' said Adorabella.

He lifted an eyebrow. 'Well, that is a very apt description; it's true, so white and smooth and plump, with the pale pink palm below.' He said suspiciously: 'What do *you* know of Miss Frere's hands?'

'Only that they are full of gold,' said Jane. 'She saw Mr. Havering dancing with the young lady last night. Why else should *he* dance with her?'

'Mr. Havering told her that he didn't like her dress,' said Dorabella. 'So she's horrid about him this morning.'

That day it rained and they sat in what had come to be called 'the school sitting-room', comfortably furnished with its old square table and solid, straight-backed chairs for working, and easy chairs where a young lady might curl up and sit lounging instead of upright and poised as in front of one's elders; its narrow piano with candle sconces and pleated green silk front. Coffee was brought in, in the fat old nursery coffee pot and the cups and saucers, sprigged with violets, that Miss Arabella had known from her childhood days. 'She'd have had me practising my scales an hour if she'd had her way with me...'

'Why did he not like your dress?' said Callie, astonished. 'I heard it so much admired.'

She was weary still and jaded, her head ached, her heart was sick. 'He thought it not suitable,' she said, shrugging. 'And indeed the whole thing was not suitable. No one has ever asked Cinderella whether she wouldn't have been safer and even happier by her fireside in the kitchen. I shall go no more into a world where I don't belong.'

'You will soon belong there of your own right,' said Dorabella, protesting. 'She had two proposals of marriage last night, Callie, she told me so and...'

'Oh, Dorabella, nonsense! I was joking. People will misunderstand.'

'And one actually from a *prétendu* of my own,' persisted Dorabella, ignoring her.

Jane looked up sharply. She recalled how Dominic had asked her if she would not like to be mistress of such an estate as his own, of how his hand had for a moment closed tightly on hers when she asked him, jesting, if this were not a proposal. She saw that Callie also was looking at her, a little startled. But Dorabella was saying easily: 'Sir Rufus John was looking down into her face with imploring tenderness. I saw him.'

'He was telling me how *you* laid waste all hearts in the neighbourhood including his own,' said Jane, thankful to have her thought deflected. And she forced a light laugh and confessed that it was a real, live Marquis who had actually been brought to a declaration. 'He assures me that his mother would welcome me, with my worsted mittens and nursery cane, to keep him in order. Oh, no, it was Sir Rufus, if that is his name as now you tell me, who expected me to have had the mittens and chalky fingers.'

'Very well—and the rest?'

'The rest is make-believe,' she said. 'In fact we need only concentrate upon the Marquis, and in him I think we shall find nothing but a somewhat ignoble mockery of one not quite in a position to reply in kind.' She knew that it had been done in the purest spirit of fun, might have been addressed to any lady of high birth; had been all a joke without thought of any inequality. But bitterness swept over her. *I fear you would find the lady not very amiable* ... 'Dear Callie,' she said, 'why would you not have danced with me? I should have been safe with you.'

'Not from a proposal, however,' said Dorabella. 'Really, Callie, it's time you were coming to the point with her.' But she recalled, perhaps, Jane's outburst and the accusation that she made a cruel mock of both, in suggesting that these two might come together. She added quickly, trying to gloss it over, to carry it all forward as the joke which in fact it had always been, without the smallest malice. 'Or you will find yourself cut out—and by the peerage.'

They were bidden to the Great House that evening. Lady Mellowes must hear all about the ball, what new offers Adorabella had received and how she had answered them; how the dress had fared and its wearer ... But would not He be there?—whose blue eyes changed all too readily from blue gleam to a glassy cold. ('A governess—and penniless.') '*I* shall not go,' she said.

Miss Ferris came into the room. The kindness of the previous evening had reverted to her everyday haughty frigidity. 'You speak in a very imperious voice, Miss Bird. Will not go—where?'

'I prefer not to call at the Great House today, Miss Ferris.'

'And who asks your preferences? You are not invited to the Great House as a guest. You are simply bidden to accompany your pupil.'

If it was harsh, it was yet the simple truth; and a salutory truth at that. Jane said, at once: 'Yes. I'm sorry. You are right, ma'am.'

'Though you may have been taken into society for one evening on an equality with your employers, there is no need to lose your head and behave for the rest of the time as though in fact you are.'

'Cousin Hannah—' began Dorabella, angrily.

Jane stopped her. 'Miss Ferris is quite right. I had forgotten it. I am paid to do my simple duty and since I accept that condition, of course I am very wrong in forgetting that I should fulfil it.' She said, trying to smile: 'I have become a little too much used to being Miss Dove —and forgotten about Miss Bird.' She spoke in genuine humility. She said: 'Miss Ferris thought it a mistake for me to go out last night, and was wiser than any of us.' And to Cousin Hannah: 'I wore your pearls with great, great pleasure in them; but I'll wear them no more for I shall go dancing no more. If therefore, I may regard them as a loan—the kindest of loans—and return them to you now, that will be best for my happiness.'

'A gift is a gift, Miss Dove,' said Callie, intervening. 'To return it is never gracious, whatever the circumstances. Miss Ferris would like you to keep the pearls. I understand her better than you do.'

'Yes, keep them,' said Miss Ferris abruptly; and left the room, saying only: 'And obey your instructions, which are no more and no less than that; you go up to the Great House with Miss Mellowes today.'

'Oh, Miss Dove, don't heed her, the cross old patch! Your duty, indeed! You shall come or go as it pleases you.'

'No, my dear, she's right; and indeed she's done me good: she speaks fairly and squarely and clears my mind when it needed it. And brings us back to our duty yet once again. Callie, if you must sit with us, don't waste our time: hear Dorabella's latest song and correct her in her upper register which I know is beyond me...'

('Will He be there? Oh, heaven, if he is there! How shall I meet his eyes, how shall I comport myself without tell-tale blushing—and what tale would the blushes tell, for I hardly know, myself? And what will he say to my missing the last dance with him?' It was all confusion; but she must go. She felt a sort of gratitude to Cousin

Hannah's rough frankness which had brought her back to her lost senses.)

The hour for calling had arrived. Charles, the footman came to the sitting-room door, bouquet in hand. 'Sir Rufus John, Miss, calling upon Miss Arabella.'

'Oh, lord!' said Dorabella. 'He calls after every ball, with flowers. Must I go down to him?'

Jane glanced at Callie for guidance. 'I'm not versed in this sort of manners. Should she go?'

'She may excuse herself,' said Callie, shrugging, 'on one pretence or other. But she ought not to. Sir Rufus is an honest fellow and he loves her; she owes him for that, at least her courtesy.'

'Well, we'll all go down, Miss Dove, and sit in the morning-room "receiving". We may as well. I daresay there will be others. Now that I think of it, there was a Mr. Greene last night, a new one, seemed very much taken. And a funny old dodderer, Earl of Somewhereor-other, positively pressing; for a moment I thought it might be Brunel. But Brunel wasn't there last night; was he?'

'No, no, his cork leg would keep him at home I daresay. Come, Dorabella, you haven't given an answer to Charles.'

'Her ladyship is in the with-drawing-room, Miss Arabella.'

'Oh, very well, Charles, show Sir Rufus in to her if you please and say we shall be down.'

Sir Rufus was there, his high colour matching his name as Adorabella thanked him deliciously for his flowers, throwing him all too evidently into an agony of hopeless devotion. And Mr. Greene was duly announced and his offering prettily accepted, and, 'Sir Edmund Welles calling upon Miss Mellowes,' and 'Lord Faversham calling upon Miss Mellowes' and 'Mr. George Bates calling upon Miss Mellowes' and 'The Marquis of Hawkfield...'

The Marquis of Hawkfield—calling upon Miss Jane Bird.

He came into the room, crowded now with gentlemen and bouquets; bowed low to Lady Mellowes who sat all enchanting smiles at the fuss and excitement on her daughter's behalf, on the pink brocade sofa. 'You will permit me, my lady? Your charming young charge last night stole my heart away...'

Jane's own heart rose. The tone of laughing banter, the fun, the twinkle, the total acceptance that she would recognise the joke between them. 'No doubt your mama, the Duchess, has sent you to recover it?' Nevertheless, she clutched the bouquet tight, and felt a naughty frisson of triumph as she saw Cousin Hannah's glance of disapproving astonishment.

'On the contrary, she sends me to endorse my importunities. Mama,' he said to Lady Mellowes, 'is bent upon my having Miss Bird to recover me from my deplorable excesses and bring me to mend my ways. She has seen no other young lady one half so capable.'

'Her ladyship's intentions are well,' suggested Jane, 'but not entirely flattering?'

'May I hasten to sweeten them by assuring you that never so charmingly have her tastes coincided with my own.'

'The only question remaining, then, is as to whether I shall make my answer to yourself or to her ladyship.'

'You have already promised it to *me* the next ball, you remember? Till then, I must possess my soul in patience.'

'At the very next ball I go to,' said Jane, 'you shall receive it.' And she smiled and dropped a kiss on to the top flower in the bouquet and thanked him for it; and moved quietly away. No one should say that she greedily lapped up even his nonsensical attentions. Sir Rufus now stood alone. She said to him, 'Alas!—I fear you have prospered no more than usual in your plans to avoid crusty bachelorhood?'

'Look around you,' he said, dolefully. 'In such company —how should *I* have a chance? Not that I ever have had any.'

She said gently, seriously now: 'Yet you must persevere? To your own constant pain and disappointment?'

'If a man is in love,' he said, turning away his head, shrugging sadly, 'he's in love. He can do nothing about it.'

'It is the same with a girl,' she said. 'We are all poor creatures together, at the mercy of hearts uncontrolled. And as you say—nothing to be done about it.'

'I shouldn't ask,' he said, 'but you seem to speak with fellow feeling?'

'And I mustn't answer. But one day far ahead when you are a crusty old bachelor, perhaps at the same time I shall be a cross old spinster; and then we will meet and I will tell you all about it.'

'I sometimes think,' he said, 'that two such sad people, you and I, or any two others—should pool their resources; should, of their pair of broken hearts build up one single heart between them—and so make something of their lives. What do you say to that?'

She quoted, smiling: 'At the very next ball we meet at—I will give you my answer,' and thought to herself: He speaks now, almost meaninglessly; but—somewhere in all this, somewhere among all these people—may there not lie an answer indeed, to all my troubles. And knew, even as she asked herself the question, that her own foolish heart, unacceptable to him who all unknowingly chained it to him—would hold her for ever from inferior consolations. And as she talked and smiled and curtsied—Miss Jane Bird in her pale, dull day-dress, very much Miss Mellowes' paid governess and companion and yet (to Cousin Hannah's patent astonishment) perfectly at ease and easily accepted by all these fine gentlemen—she

125

thought all the time: 'I am to go to the Great House tonight. Will He be there?'

He was not there. He had gone, said Sir Dermot crossly, to take his dinner in Robinstown. 'He has some friend, I don't know who, a Mr. Yallerdor or some such name; never heard of him myself, not anyone of our acquaintance, certainly. Some rakish companion, I suppose, and my young gentleman must be off every now and again to spend an evening with him. Or an afternoon or even a morning—Mr. Yallerdor seems very free of his time. Much freer than Master Richard Havering need be, for my part.'

'Well, my dear, he's a young creature, you cannot hold him every moment in your fusty old researchings.'

'Yallerdor?' said Callie. 'A curious name,'—and suddenly looked up, as though an inspiration came to him and one not very much welcome. Jane intercepted a swift flash of communication between himself and Miss Ferris who also had raised her head sharply from a moment's brown study. For Miss Ferris, too, had seen the gentleman disappearing into the house with the yellow door. Mr. Havering was going his own ways, it seemed; and poking gentle private fun as he did so, at those unaware of his secrets. ('*I have heard him say—a little in his cups —that he goes there to see a lady—or keeps a lady there, that was the way of it, I now remember.*') The lady was young and beautiful, the speaker had said, confiding it all in an undertone to Callie, that day at the emporium; and a foreigner. The Yallerdor visited by Mr. Richard Havering was the yellow door of a house in Capsicum Street.

Dorabella chattered through the dinner hour to her Aunt Mellowes of the glories of the ball, of her own enjoyment, of the latest new suitor—whom she spoke of with genuine detachment, one of too many that had come her heedless way, to evoke any interest, save that he had at least not a wooden leg. Jane remained silent. 'I am in my dove-grey again,' she reminded herself, 'I am here by command, as Miss Mellowes'—servant.' The reflection was without bitterness; a position sought and thankfully accepted. 'It is only when I am among others that I grow proud and suffer,' she thought: 'who may look down upon me. Here no one looks down on me; they accept my position, what else?—and I, who applied for it and was thankful to get it, must accept it also and behave accordingly.' If she did not like that, she should remove herself from the situation. It was perhaps a little their fault, she reflected—their kindly fault—in allowing her, in urging her, to step out of her place. Their fault—partly: all her own if she did not, without rancour, return to it. She answered Lady Mellowes' enquiries demurely. Yes, she had very much enjoyed the evening; but had grown very tired towards the end—was not accustomed to late nights and excitement.

'So you had at least some excitement?—though you speak of it with so little colour.'

'I am Miss Bird again today, my lady; in my colourless dress. And very happy,' said Jane, with quiet meaning, 'back here in my dove-côte.'

'Don't heed her, Aunt! She had two proposals last night. And I think from this morning's observation that even my wearisome adorer, Sir Rufus, is going over to the enemy. The belovèd enemy,' said Dorabella, quickly; ever returning in her mind to the storm that had blown up over those earlier accusations, too carelessly, and a little too meaningfully levelled. 'You are welcome to him, Miss Dove, with all my heart!'

'You watch me very closely,' said Jane, careful to echo her mood of amicable teasing. 'And always to no purpose. Once more, the poor gentleman was but bemoaning his fate to me.' She did not add that he had hinted, however little he may have meant it, at a means of easing it.

'Two proposals?' said Lady Mellowes, a little probing.

'Well, so she boasts; though when it comes to it she can produce only one firm offer. That, however,' said Dorabella, all mischievous laughter, 'was from a Marquis.'

'Who, nevertheless, positively called upon her this morning,' said the Dowager, with her indulgent smile.

'In jest, my lady. It is all a piece of nonsense. And this wicked girl mocks me—me and my two proposals!'

'Still—what marquis called upon you?'

'It was but Lord Chalmers of Hawkfield, cousin; a monstrous rake with the women,' put in Hannah Ferris, tossing back the lock of hair. 'And now runs after a governess.'

'It is *as* a governess that he runs after me, ma'am,' said Jane, refusing to be offended. 'He declares that I shall reform him; and that my lady, the Duchess, believes it too.'

'She might not be far wrong,' said old Lady Mellowes. 'We know that you can be a determined young person. But beware, my child, for it's true that Chalmers is a wicked fellow; though not, I have always thought, a bad one.'

'At any rate, my lady, he is very safe from *my* governessing.'

'That I quite appreciate,' said old Lady Mellowes; and looked her very straitly in the eye, as though to say: 'I know who is *your* foolish preference.' 'And there I may place myself in what danger I will, for all she cares,' thought Jane; 'if it will but release Miss Arabella to fulfil the destiny designed for her.'

The weather cleared and on the following afternoon Adorabella would go riding. Callie, calling with some message for the Dowager had mentioned carelessly that after his day's idleness Havering had his nose very firmly to the grindstone; nor did the work seem likely to entail a visit to the tapestry. 'No use going down by the bridal path, then. We'll go across the river and into the woodland on the other side; you haven't yet been there.'

'Lord Brunel's woods?'

'In name. We all consider them ours in fact. After all —a wager!'

'A wager must be honoured as faithfully as any other debt. Many young gentlemen would not otherwise be so impoverished as they appear to be, despite respectable families.'

'You're tilting at Richard. It's true that he gambled a fortune—'

'A fortune?' said Jane, surprised. 'I hadn't known that?'

'Oh, yes. He told me so himself. Well—his fortune: I don't know if that means quite the same thing. A fortune suggests some immensity. But "his" fortune might mean merely a competency. At any rate, his fortune was the way he expressed it. Left him by his father who died some three or four years ago.'

'Is his mother still living?'

'No, she was long an invalid and died shortly before his father. I think there was no Place—he makes no pretensions to aristocracy: merely a house where they lived, and whatever they lived upon ... Richard sold it all when his father died. He was very much devoted to his mother and didn't want to continue where nothing was left but sad memories. Then he went abroad to pursue his interest in the arts—'

'And to stake and lose his fortune?'

'Well, so it would seem; since we find him working as an employee of my Uncle Dermot. Still, it brought him to the Great House,' said Dorabella, comfortably, 'and the tapestry brings him here to the Dower House; so one of us at least is not complaining.' And she added with naughty complacency that she thought he didn't too bitterly complain of it either. 'Well, come—shall we ride? And Mama also, we will invite her—she shouldn't sit all the time bored and drooping with that bleak Cousin Hannah.'

Lady Mellowes acquiesced very readily; had thought of proposing it herself. A man was sent up to the Great

House to request the loan of a pretty mare, Silver, which she was accustomed to borrow for riding; she kept no stable of her own, except for her carriage horses and Dorabella's little chestnut.

They ambled down the gravelled sweep, turned on to the water meadows, crossed the bridge, entered into Brunel woodland. It was very lovely there. The old dried winter leaves, soaked by the past days of rain, chuffed softly beneath the horses' hooves, bluebells breathed their soft haze beneath the tall trees, the bridle path was edged all along with the small pale blossoms of springtime. Dorabella rode, as usual, her little chestnut, Majority; Jane had sent back the dapple grey to the Great House stable with thanks, and returned to the mettlesome Aldebaran. 'You are kindness itself,' she had said to Dominic Mellowes, still professing some concern, 'but I'm not yet quite ready for my bath-chair; and Honeycomb, you must admit, though as sweet as her name, is something of a bath-chair.'

'It was Dorabella who was anxious for you,' said Dominic; and as the young lady herself appeared, 'I am telling Miss Bird that we are worried about her riding that great, pulling bay of ours...'

Dorabella's fears seemed suddenly considerably abated. 'Oh, she'll do well enough on him, she can easily handle him.' Her own hands, she said, spreading them out before her with a somewhat apparent pretence at ruefulness, were too foolishly small to control a big heavy horse. Jane was much the stronger rider. Jane meekly accepted this decidedly backhand compliment, the more so as it elicited a broad, amused wink from Callie. 'At any rate, you'll trust me, Mr. Mellowes? Aldebaran and I will take good care of one another.'

But now the bay was certainly a little difficult, prancing sideways, barging against the other two, tossing his handsome head, longing to be off and away and stretch his splendid legs. 'They are all fretful after the rain that has kept them so long without exercise,' said Dorabella, for even Majority was dancing a little impatiently and the quiet Silver rolled back her eyes at the impatient curvettings of her companions. 'When we come through the woods to the grass again, we'll let them out in a good, hard gallop.'

'We had better turn back before then, Dorabella. We're already trespassing on Lord Brunel's territory.'

'Oh, but Mama, would you miss the chance of an encounter? How if I lose all constraint and Majority flings me from the saddle—to fall in a graceful heap, at old Hoppity's door! So that he may lift me in his arms—no, no, he's past any such exercise!—so that he may summon his minions, then—to lift and carry me into his ogre's castle; and so, watching over the couch where I lie, pale as a broken lily—fall in love with me in that one romantic moment and offer me back the stolen Mellowes acres, lock, stock, mud and all....' And in her laughing excitement, she dug her little heels into the chestnut's flanks; and he broke from her light, restraining grip and laid back his ears and fairly bolted with her up the long avenue...

Jane gave the big bay his head and went after her.

She thought afterwards that it had been perhaps a foolish move; yet what else should she have done, how could she have known that the corridor through the woods would be so long?—the chestnut fleeing all the faster from the great hooves thundering after him. She saw that Dorabella was quite out of control, swaying in the sidesaddle like a helpless flower in her velvet habit, the feathered hat tumbled off and the auburn hair streaming back in a wild tangle of curls as she tugged unavailingly at the reins. Faster and faster! 'Edge him to one side!' screamed Jane, trying to come up alongside her and so catch at the reins nearer the bit and ease down the pace; but the path grew narrower, the closer she came to the chestnut's flank, the more her own horse must bore against him, driving him frantically on. Behind her she heard

Lady Mellowes close but ever losing ground: glanced back and saw the slight figure, gallantly riding, urging on the silver mare. 'We come out on to grass meadow-land,' she thought. 'What will happen then?'—and had no time to recall the laughing description of Adorabella's graceful descent at Lord Brunel's door.

And at last—at the end of the tunnel of trees—light: rough grass, angled by woodland. The chestnut made no check, streamed across it; but now she could bring up the bay, could reach out to snatch at Majority's bridle. The little horse reared: spun round, and started, but at a less violent pace, cornerwise across the field. The silver mare appeared at the mouth of the bridle path and gave chase. The chestnut checked once more, turned its head and, with Dorabella still clinging to the pommel, disappeared down the path back into the woods through which they had come: and the bay, Aldebaran, loudly whinnying, rose up on his hind legs, pawing the air in rage and bafflement at being so suddenly brought up, all standing, in the midst of his unchecked gallop; fell back, bringing his rider with him, scrambled to his feet again and, all passion spent, stood quietly looking down at her.

Lady Mellowes wrenched at her rein and came flying up on her silver mare; slipped from the saddle, knelt beside her. Jane opened her eyes. 'I'm all right ... Just—shaken...' And raised her head to see, with dull eyes, that a rider had broken out from the far corner of the woods and was dashing over towards them.

He halted his horse, leapt down. Lady Mellowes got back to her feet. She said urgently: 'Look after her! Help me up, and you stay here and look after her!' He asked no questions, held a hand; she put one light foot into it and was up and into the saddle and had turned and was scorching back across the field and into the bridle path after the flying chestnut.

A tall, lean figure, dark haired, without the smallest streak of grey. A fine nose, high arched; keen grey eyes;

strong white hands, lifting her to lie against an encircling arm. Jane looked up and into the face of the famous Lord Brunel.

'Don't try to move,' he said. 'Tell me first—are you injured, have you any pain?'

She said again: 'Only shaken.'

'What happened?'

'The horse reared and fell back and I with it.' She raised her head to look about her. 'Is he all right? My horse—?'

'Like yourself—only shaken. Now,' he said, looking down at her, 'what are we to do with you?'

'If you would be so good as to see me home to the Dower House...'

'The Dower House?'

'Please, yes—to the Dower House.' But as she scrambled back to her feet, she came near to fainting. 'You're not yet strong enough,' he said, anxiously.

'Yes ... If you please...' She must know what had happened, if Adorabella was safe. 'If you would help me mount—?'

He lifted her into the saddle, not with a hand to her boot-sole as he had Lady Mellowes, but with both hands at her waist and a lift and a jump; mounted his own horse and slowly rode back with her along the bridle path, the horses close, both reins gathered into one strong hand, the other arm round her, supporting her. Along the path, across the meadows, up the gravelled drive. She lifted her head and saw that the chestnut was being led away quietly to the stables, that a groom had mounted the silver and was riding down to meet them. It would seem then, that all must be well; there was no commotion at the door, there could have been no time for any serious accident to occur which now there was no signs of. She relaxed against the strong arm. When the groom approached she lifted weary eyes and said: 'I'm quite all right, Stone.' And, feebly smiling: 'Just a little battered.'

'They say you were very brave, Miss.'

'She has been very brave,' said Lord Brunel. He rode with her up to the front door steps, lifted her down, gently; held her still against his arm, strong and comforting. Cousin Hannah came hurrying down the steps, followed by the Dowager. He relaxed his hold immediately, sufficiently at any rate to bow coldly to both. 'Miss Ferris? Lady Mellowes!'

'Lord Brunel! Oh, thank you! But is she all right?' cried the little Dowager, anxiously fluttering.

'No serious damage. Shocked and I daresay somewhat bruised...'

Two footmen had come down and he handed her over to their support. Lady Mellowes said, all too clearly longing to go back with her into the house and be assured that all was well: 'Will you not come in, and allow me to thank you properly?'

'Thank you, no,' he said, in his cold way. 'I am sure you are anxious to be released.' He bowed farewells. 'Only too happy to have been of assistance.'

'As indeed you have been—and a thousand thanks to you. Perhaps you will call tomorrow?' she asked, almost wistfully, chilled by his coldness yet eager to seem all appreciation, 'and see how the patient fares. And allow us then to express our gratitude with more composure?'

He bowed again, wordlessly: took the reins from the groom standing holding his horse, gathered them up where the fine, flowing mane met the shoulder, without assistance put a foot in the stirrup and leapt up into the saddle: and with a last civil flourish of his riding hat, moved off down the drive. 'But what in the world can we have done to offend him?' murmured the poor little Dowager, gazing after him.

On the next afternoon, however, he called. 'Lord Brunel my lady, to enquire after Miss Mellowes.'

They were gathered in the morning room where Jane

might lie on the comfortable couch, Dorabella at her feet, living ever over again the adventure and the meeting with the famous Lord Brunel. 'What, *riding*? You promise me? One leg each for either stirrup? It was cork, Mama, Callie always said it was cork, such wonderful things as they do now; a cork leg with a riding boot attached to look well, astride a horse...'

'He managed very steadily on it, standing there supporting our precious Miss Dove.' (Miss Dove!—who had saved her darling's life, the gallant, the selfless, the magnificently resourceful Miss Dove!—nothing could exceed the grateful mother's praise and admiration.)

'And handsome, you say, Miss Dove? Positively handsome?'

'Beautiful as a Greek god to me, at any rate,' said Jane. 'Poor battered, bruised thing that I was, wallowing in the mud, helpless.'

'I thought it best, my dear, since he was there, stronger than I—to leave you to him, and myself go after Dorabella.'

'Dear Mama, we all know you did wisely. Though by the time you came up with me,' said Dorabella, complacently, 'I had Majority back under control.'

'He was capable of control from the moment Miss Dove had checked him.'

'Oh, I take nothing from my dear Miss Dove. What might not have happened? I am ever, ever grateful to you, my dear, dear Miss Dove.' Not but what, said Adorabella, a graceful fall at his lordship's door as originally planned might have been yet more romantic.

'He seemed so strangely cold and—unfriendly. He was always a proud man,' said Lady Mellowes, 'and perhaps, looking back on it, rather haughty and reserved. Of course that was ten years ago or twelve, before his wife died and he went off abroad.'

'Has he never been back since then?'

'Only for short spells, presumably to see to his affairs

here. But on those occasions we haven't seen him.'

'I was too young then to be sacrificed on the altar, Miss Dove, you see. So no attempt was made to lure him into the net. Now, however, rumour assures us he returns for good.'

'Nobody is sacrificing you, Arabella,' said Miss Ferris impatiently; and: 'If such a marriage were to promise your happiness, dearest, of course the family would very much welcome it. However, after his chilly demeanour yesterday,' said Lady Mellowes, shrugging rather helplessly, 'it looks unlikely that we shall see any more of him.'

And the footman was at the door. 'Lord Brunel to enquire after Miss Mellowes.'

Cousin Hannah exchanged a somewhat startled glance with her ladyship, rose and went out into the hall. They could hear her clear, carrying voice. 'To save embarrassment … Perhaps your lordship is not aware … We are none the less grateful; but the young lady concerned was not Miss Mellowes but Miss Mellowes' companion and governess.'

A brief silence. Then the measured tones: a touch of sarcasm? 'In that case, I will give myself if I may, the satisfaction of reassuring myself as to the well-being of Miss Mellowes' companion and governess.'

'Oh, certainly! Lady Mellowes will be delighted to receive you.' And he was in the room, bowing in that cold, haughty way of his: very tall, as Jane had remembered him with the long, handsome face, fine nose and keen, brilliant grey eyes. Lady Mellowes rose to curtsey, Dorabella, obviously somewhat taken aback by his fine figure and handsome good looks, also curtsied prettily, a little pink in her confusion. Jane was struggling up from the sofa but he held up his hand. 'Remain where you are I beg; or I shall be obliged to retire and incommode you no further.'

'Yes, stay, Miss Dove. May I present,' said Lady Mellowes with a graceful gesture of her tiny hand, 'our little friend Miss Bird—the more valued now than ever, as your lordship will suppose, since her gallant rescue yesterday, of my daughter.'

He bowed; his eyebrows asked permission, he drew up a chair, placed it close to Jane's couch. 'I hope I find you not too much shaken by your experience?'

'No, indeed, my lord; and must offer you my best thanks for all your assistance.'

'I should be interested to learn the whole story. Miss Bird had come to the rescue of Miss Mellowes—?' He glanced towards Adorabella and, apparently with very little interest in that young lady's charms, looked back to Jane. Jane cast a glance of appeal towards Lady Mellowes.

'My daughter's horse bolted. Miss Bird went after her and in contriving to check her horse, brought her own up short: which reared and fell back on her.'

'It was at that moment that my attention was attracted.' He said, addressing Jane directly: 'You had a narrow escape.'

'But escaped. It was Miss Mellowes, perhaps,' said Jane, trying vainly to attract his attention elsewhere, 'who in the end had the worst of it...'

'Why no, for what did I have but a good gallop through Lord Brunel's woods, once across his field and so back home again? It was Mama had the worst fright of all— torn between two imperative duties.'

'Perhaps,' said Lady Mellowes, in her pretty, dimply way, 'Lord Brunel will say that it serves us all right, for trespassing.'

At once he scraped back his chair and rose to his feet. 'Your ladyship and Miss Mellowes are naturally most welcome to ride wherever you will.' And he bowed again and wished Miss Bird a speedy recovery and, as Dorabella said the moment he had gone, all but stalked out of the room. 'Well! The very personification of pride!' However, she confessed, by no means unhandsome. 'And conceals the cork leg very well. I begin to quite dote on him.'

'Too late, alas,' said Lady Mellowes, pretending a sigh. 'For I think this really is the last time we shall see him.'

He called again the next day, nevertheless. Miss Bird was well enough to be out walking in the ground with her pupil. She must be very much recovered, he said; but on the next day called yet again to make quite sure of it.

There was much jubilation at the Great House. 'With all respect to you, dear Miss Bird—I wonder, Rose-abelle, if he does not in fact come to see Arabella?'

'He never looks my way,' said Dorabella, ruefully. 'Not that I wish him to, poor old thing, with his glass eye and all that concealed cork; but it would be more flattering.'

'I daresay you make not the smallest effort to attract him?'

'On the contrary, Aunt, I am one alluring smile from ear to ear and chattering like a magpie. We even contrived one day that he should interrupt my singing. He simply sat silent and at the end managed to bring into the conversation that he did not care for music. "Even when it was good," he did not outwardly add.'

An invitation to dine went forth from the Great House but his lordship was desolated that previous engagements would prevent his attending—on that or any date his tone might well imply. 'You had better ask him to the Dower House then, Rose-abelle. He must by now be running out of excuses for calling.'

'It's all of no use, my dear aunt, he won't marry me, not even if we all go down on our bended knees to him. Though upon reflection,' said Adorabella, 'may this not be the explanation? How can he kneel to beg my hand with the creak of the wooden leg preventing him?'

Lord Brunel, though so much occupied at other times, was able to declare himself free to accept for the party at the Dower House. 'There!' said old Lady Mellowes, triumphant. 'Let them but meet on such occasions, here and there about the county, let him see how much she is admired...'

And indeed a small rash of entertaining appeared to be springing up in a neighbourhood hitherto rather quiet at this particular season: arising largely, it seemed, from the spring-board of the Aurora Baines ball. Mr. Foster proposed a large luncheon, and hoped Lady Mellowes would permit him to include in his invitation her charming friend, Miss Bird. Sir Frederick Travenne was giving a dinner and his invitation included the name of Miss Bird. And the Duchess of Grantham was giving a dance, and the Marquis, her son, had particularly desired her to extend her invitation to Miss Bird ... Lady Mellowes sent for Jane to come to her boudoir one morning. 'Our dove appears to have been winging its little way almost disconcertingly through the hearts of the county families.' Gilt-edged cards were spread over the little table. 'Sit down, my dear, and let us just talk things over.'

'I am resolved to accept no more entertainment. Your ladyship will support me when I say that I truly prefer not to?'

'Well—I think that perhaps you are wise, my dear. But ... Sir Frederick Travenne seems—a little particular. He writes me a note saying that while he of course does not wish to press for it, he has—what's his phrase?—has mentioned your name to his sister (who lives with him, you know) and would like to present you to her.' She looked at Jane consideringly. 'This is very kind, I think? And Sir Frederick is in perhaps a special situation. You might feel more free to accept—?'

Jane recalled with shame the outward indifference with which she must have appeared to receive his offer of future help, so delicately expressed; she had been intent upon the conversation overheard between Richard Havering and the two other men, and had hardly replied. Would this be perhaps the time to make amends? 'If your ladyship thinks ... If I may wear my plain governess-dress,' decided Jane, 'perhaps I might go to the grange. Just that one occasion, if you would not object to it?'

So the days went by and Miss Bird stayed safe at home. Mr. Foster's luncheon was charming, and Adorabella sat next to Lord Charles Wembleydale and everyone was sure that he was much attracted to her—but Miss Bird stayed safe at home. And the Duchess's 'little dance' took place, but Miss Bird stayed home. The party at the grange must unhappily be postponed on account of the temporary illness—a recurrent affair—of Sir Frederick Travenne; so even as to that Miss Bird stayed at home ...

And Lord Brunel consented at last—to a dinner at the Dower House; but Miss Bird remained in her own room. 'You had much better have come down, Miss Dove, all the same,' said Arabella as the ladies sat over the teacups on the following afternoon, describing the occasion to Lady Mellowes, up at the Great House. 'At least he might have uttered a word or two to *you*. As it was, he sat proud as a poker, did he not, Mama?—bowed stiffly when addressed, replied in two words and retired back into the ivory tower of unrelenting grandeur.'

Lady Mellowes looked somewhat unhappily at the dowager for confirmation and received a rueful nod. Jane said: 'If even with your family he's so proud, Dorabella, he's not very likely to have unbent for the governess.'

'He did so agreeably enough in those days when he came enquiring after your health, following the accident.'

'He was doing precisely that—enquiring after my health, following the accident. He can hardly have maintained his interest in my bruises as long as this!'

'Miss Bird is quite right, Arabella.'

'Just the same, Aunt, he enquired after her very tenderly; and I dare say wondered at it, that she was not present.'

'If he's as haughty as you say,' said Jane, laughing, 'he's not likely to have expected to be invited to meet the governess.'

'I did suggest that you come down,' said the Dowager, ever concerned not to wound. 'But you would not.'

'Indeed, my lady, you know I don't expect to be asked. I much, much prefer things as they are.'

The footman was dismissed, Lady Mellowes poured tea, Jane assisted Miss Ferris in handing round cups, sugar and cream. 'Anyway,' said Adorabella, 'I fear Aunt, that you must give up all hopes of me. He thinks nothing of me whatsoever; except that he may have sufficiently glanced in my direction to observe that I was young, and from that would conclude that I must, of my very nature, be tiresome and uninteresting.'

'Did you make any effort to suggest otherwise?'

Dorabella sat curled up on a footstool at her mother's knee. 'Why indeed I did, did I not, Mama? Support me! I was dressed to the nines, my pale blue silk, Aunt, what could be more alluring? with Mama's little diamond necklace lent for the occasion—'

'And indeed, looked a picture, Sister: like a creature of the water, in the pale blue, with these droplets around her neck...'

'But all in vain. You can bring a horse to the water, droplets and all, but he will not drink. I smiled and curtsied and shook my curls at him till I thought they would fall off into the soup; but not a word spoke he. The truth is,' said Dorabella, 'that he has not only a wooden leg beneath those exquisitely fitting unmentionables of his but a wooden spine also that renders him so unbending.'

'I suppose you were foolish and silly, coquetting like a callow schoolroom miss instead of speaking quietly and sensibly?'

'No, Sister, I must defend her; she behaved very charmingly.'

'Why should I not? The cork leg is well concealed and for the rest he is, for a dotard, highly personable; moreover, the air of reserve is a challenge, one so longs to break it down and *force* him into admiration.'

'This is a serious matter, my child, you know. No one co-erces you; but to be mistress of that great Brunel mansion, is not nothing—'

'Not to mention of the Brunel acres which really and truly are the Robinsford acres, as we all know ...'

'When you have a little grown up,' said Cousin Hannah, 'you will appreciate these things, Arabella. Not to do so, only shows you to be still childish and silly. To be a very great lady in a county such as this, is an honour which brings with it many, many benefits as one grows older. You'd take precedence everywhere—except of course of the Duchess—'

'And of the Marchioness. Miss Dove, when you were the Marchioness of Hawkfield you would walk in to dinner ahead of me! And when we were both old and you Duchess in your turn, I should still be merely Lady Brunel and your very daughters-in-law would march before me ... No, Cousin Hannah, it really isn't worth the cork and that formidable glass eye.'

'Lord Brunel has no glass eye—'

'He might just as well have two, the way he uses them. And glass they must be, surely, if they see no charms in all my efforts to please, for indeed I hop about like a little trained monkey, shaking my curls at him, mouthing and ogling him, chatter, chatter, chatter—now do I not, Mama?'

'It is in your hands to please him Arabella.'

'But I tell you, dearest Aunt, he will not be pleased! He takes no notice of all my pretty gibberings. I think I never tried harder with a man in my life.'

'I hope indeed that you do not "try" with any gentle-men!'

'What have you just been exhorting me to do with Lord Brunel?'

Lady Mellowes handed her cup to Cousin Hannah for re-filling. 'It will be most bitterly disappointing, Rose-abelle,

142

if this—arrangement—does not come about. Who else in the family...? She is our only hope. If he marries again, elsewhere, the land is gone for ever. A quiverful of boys—'

'What, Aunt, at his age? And with a woo-...'

'Dorabella—you are indelicate!'

'I only say, Mama, that a quiverful of—of walking-sticks would be more likely. And indeed,' said Dorabella, bursting into giggles, 'most suitable, as props in his imminent old age.'

'Miss Dove—take her away; she is incorrigible,' said her mother, trying to conceal her own laughter.

'Yes, lovey-Dovey, let's go down to the stables. Who knows but we may find his lordship there, "enquiring after Aldebaran's health, following upon the accident". If *you* are with me,' said Dorabella, gaily, 'he may talk to us. He was all charm and kindness, when he came to visit *you*.'

They were more likely to meet the young gentlemen and there indeed were Dominic and Callie in great anxiety about the lameness of a favourite carriage horse. 'If I can get no attention but by hopping on one foot,' said Dorabella, at last, 'we will go home. I see that it is useless to try to compete with Handsome.'

'Handsome is as Handsome does,' said Callie, apologetically, 'and he does very ill at the moment. Even Sir Dermot is leaving his papers to come and look at him.' Sir Dermot was, in fact, a considerable expert on horseflesh; and what was more, where Sir Dermot went so was Richard Havering likely to come. 'Well, we will not desert so interesting an invalid,' said Adorabella, 'till we've heard the last opinion.'

Richard came. Bowed to Adorabella, suddenly all smiles: kissed her little hand, though not in that special place between the glove and the cuff; bowed somewhat coolly to her companion. She had not seen him to speak to since the night of the ball. 'I hope I see Miss Bird quite recovered?'

'I suffered a few bruises, that was all. I thank you.'

'I referred to an earlier indisposition. You were too unwell, when last we met, to make good your promise of the final dance with me.'

'That was a long time ago. I have had ample time to get better.'

'I, alas!—don't recover so easily,' he said, bowing.

The stables were by no means the least beautiful part of Robinsford: a great, cobbled, walled-in yard, lined with white-painted stalls, each crested with the name of its inhabitant: the gentle heads poked out inquisitively as Handsome was slowly paraded on his patch of specially laid down straw, standing still at last, patiently, while the hoof was upturned for examination. Dorabella, brought up all her life with horses, crowded in with the men, to look. For a moment, Jane was left standing with Richard Havering, a little apart. His tone of light banter altered. 'You were not very kind to desert me that night,' he said.

'As to kindness,' she said sharply, 'we won't enter into competition.'

'I—have ever been unkind to *you*?'

She took a resolution. Mysteries were foolish, filled with the temptation of bitter little hints and dark allusions. It was better to come out into the open, painful though it might be, and somehow final. She said: 'Mr. Havering— it need not matter to you, but for my own peace of mind and future conduct, I had better tell you this frankly. Out on the terrace that night, I unwillingly overheard references to myself—which I think may end even any mock pretence at friendship between us. We must preserve the civilities of course—'

He broke in upon her. He had gone rather white. 'You overheard? Very well, it is painful but I must explain myself. Your appearance was such that evening as to attract attention—not always from desirable quarters. Certain gentlemen enquired of me as to your—condition.'

'As it might be after Handsome's hoof?'

'They asked me, if you will have it plain, whether or not you might be worth their pursuit.'

'You would naturally assume that to be from the point of view of any fortune.'

'In the case of these particular gentlemen, yes.'

'They couldn't have applied to a better source,' she said bitterly.

He stood straight and tall before her. The sunshine beat down upon his fair head, the handsome face was bent to look down into hers, the blue eyes now were clouded. Her own eyes wavered before the intentness of his gaze. He said at last, low voiced: 'You have a very low opinion of me, Miss Bird.'

She turned away her head. She said, wretchedly: 'I have been taught to—to—'

'Ah, taught,' he said. 'By others?'

'By my own observation.'

'And this episode confirms it?' He said impatiently, almost angrily: 'Two objectionable men approached me, not, as you seem to believe, as an expert in such matters but as a friend of the Mellowes family who had introduced you to the ball. Rather than subject you to their attentions, I told them sharply that you had no fortune—'

'Being merely a governess?'

'You were telling everybody that yourself. To tell them so, was to finish entirely their most undesirable pretensions to your acquaintance. They might not have believed my protestations as to fortune—'

She knew herself foolish, unwise; indeed unfair. But she had been deeply wounded and now could not hold back the bitterness. 'Supposing you to be after that yourself?'

He checked. His mouth took a grim line, she thought that he would turn and walk away, return to the group about the horse. 'And it would serve me right,' she thought. 'Why can't I beat down my pride?—why must I fight back so savagely when I find it wounded?—why must I sacrifice to it, even those smiles, even that look of his that, though in fact it means so little, means so much to *me*?' But he relaxed. He said, as though with an effort: '*You* can hardly suppose that, however?'

She was confused, could not quite believe her ears, could not accept, certainly, what the words might seem to import. She stammered: 'I neither—neither so flatter nor demean myself as to suppose you to be "after" anyone so little "amiable" as myself; fortune or no fortune.'

Now the blue eyes blazed into hers, the mouth grew grim again and relaxed no more. 'Your mind is so firmly fixed upon fortune-hunting, Madam, that you are blind to any other reason for the pursuit of young ladies. However, that is not something a gentleman may discuss with you; and since you seem determined upon ill-will and misunderstanding, I can only bow to your preference. I will trouble—demean—you no further.' Handsome was being led away to his stable, the group was dissolving; he walked off and joined them. Adorabella was all reassurance, she was sure the horse had but picked up a sharp stone and cut the soft flesh behind the hoof. 'I've seen it happen before. You recall, Dommie, when Morning Glory—?'

'I think you're right. The stone is cast, leaving no other sign of its presence. The simplest explanation is often the true one,' said Dominic.

'But for one reason or another, not always the one accepted,' said Richard and walked back to the house between the two of them, without a backward glance.

Callie walked with Jane. 'Shall we take a little detour and look in on the Chinese pheasants? You are in need of some respite, I think, before we rejoin the company; and the pheasants are such colourful, brilliant birds—the very sight of them may lift up one's heart.'

She put her hand in his arm. 'Oh, Callie! I wish I had never had my one poor hour as a colourful, brilliant bird. It has done very little, indeed, to lift up *my* heart.'

'Poor little shining dove; I know!' he said.

'You are so kind and good, Callie. You observe every-thing.'

'I observe that you are in love, my dear; and suffering.'

'Dear heaven!' she said. 'Is it so apparent as that?'

'Only to hearts in the same case,' said Callie; and smiled at her and said no more.

Chapter 8

And the weeks passed and it was summer; and Sir
Frederick Travenne was recovered and would revive plans
for his party. Now an *al fresco* feast was planned, long
tables laid out on the terrace, lantern lit, his widowed
sister, Lady Fielding, playing hostess. She received Jane
very kindly. 'My brother has spoken to me of you. I am so
very glad that you would come. Enjoy your evening!'

Jane wore no pigeon's-breast gown that night, shining
blue and green: only the silvery grey-brown, with the
sheen that had—now, so long ago, it seemed—led Adorabella to christen her 'the shining dove'. So long ago!—so
long a time of pleasure and pain, of quiet happiness, of
kindness and fond affection, of work and play, a gradual
soothing of the wounded spirit that had come, via the
grim years with the old, unyielding aunt, into this deeply
resented 'servitude'—which had proved so kindly a bourne
of graciousness and ease. Of pleasure—and pain. The pain
had been all of her own making; nowadays this she knew
—that fierce pride which, offended, broke forth into anger
and sharp words too little controlled. Let her pride only
seem to be assailed and she had flown to its defence in a
counter-move often out of all proportion to the offence;
and that offence almost invariably unintended. And by so
doing...

By so doing had alienated for ever even such small joy
as her heart had fed upon, in the kindness of that voice

and the gleam of those blue, blue eyes. Since the day in the stables, he had not spoken to her again with more than the bare civility of open social exchange.

But now ... But now she was, just for this lovely evening, with one who had understood all her soreness, with one who had shared with her 'an irrational humility'; with one who had said that her situation was indeed not worthy of 'so deep and delicate a spirit'. She walked with Sir Frederick Travenne across the fairy-lit lawns. All about the gardens, the trees and bushes were hung with little packages containing gifts, and the younger guests might wander in couples, each in search of his own. 'It is all an excuse,' he said to Jane, 'to come limping with you, looking for yours; though I, of course, know very well where it is. Not that I shall cheat,' he promised, smiling. 'Naturally, the longer you take to find it, the more delightful for me!' He had up to now been occupied with other guests. 'But I hope you have been contented so far?'

'Very much so. I came, you see, in my own plain dress as my own plain self. There could be no misunderstandings—and so I have been content, and I suppose others too.'

'You were beautiful in your ball gown,' he said. 'But perhaps the shining silver-grey is best.'

(I love you best in your own soft browns and greys. Another voice had said that: a hundred aeons of sad memories ago.)

'I refused to come any other way dressed. Indeed, I've refused ever since that night, to step out of my own safe sphere. But I knew that I might come here, and since I came as a governess, dressed as a governess, in Lady Mellowes' train, and have for the most part stayed close by her side, merely a spectator—I've been very happy and content. And it's such a lovely place!'

'You won't ever forget that, in time of trouble, it would offer you refuge? That I hope was a bargain between us?'

She told a little fib. 'I was too much moved by your kindness at the time, to express to you how truly I appreciated it.'

'I have mentioned it to my sister; I'm sure you will have felt that she gave you this evening, a rather special greeting?' He said hastily: 'I hope you won't suppose that we enter into any competition in kindness with Lady Mellowes. Nothing, I'm sure, could exceed her own.'

'No indeed. But even so, there has been a time, Sir Frederick, when just to have known of this refuge would have been of untold value to me; and it's of untold value just to know it is there.'

'When we find your gift for this evening,' he said, 'you will have my pledge, so that you may never forget.'

All about them, young couples wandered and, out of distinct view of the chaperones, linked hands, perhaps, perhaps stood in the shadow of a branch and for a moment kissed and clung. 'It's very sweet to see them,' he said, walking beside her, bearing more heavily since his illness upon his amber cane. 'They are too much kept apart from life—these young girls who will one day be pitched into marriage with a man whose lightest embrace they have never known, whom they have often never so much as talked to intimately and alone. What more harm can come of a kiss exchanged, than may well come of a longing unfulfilled, for that kiss? How many have married simply because they longed to know what the kisses of this man or this girl would do for them; only to discover too late what, perhaps, an evening like this might have taught them: that the kisses didn't mean what kisses between lovers should mean—that they had better kiss elsewhere and try again.'

They walked in silence a moment. Then she said: 'Do you speak generally? Or is perhaps some of this directed towards me, personally?'

'Does some of it apply to you?'

'I wonder,' she said, rather wistfully. 'Perhaps I don't know, myself.'

He took her hand for a moment, letting go of it again, immediately. 'Well—I am an observer; having no alternative in my life. And so it's true, perhaps, that I'm not unaware of where your kisses would be disposed, if you had the choice. Whether or not they would be happily so disposed—how can I tell? And I must not dabble in the delicate realms of the safety of a young lady's heart. It's only as to her general safety that I dare interfere.' And they came to a tall tree, upon whose bough hung a package held by a silver ribbon. 'By an extraordinary coincidence,' he said laughing, 'we have come upon your gift!'

A pretty little box of painted china that tinkled a tune when she opened it. 'This is for show,' he said. 'The real gift is within; but that you shall keep to yourself, or questions will be asked and I would not have you mortified or embarrassed. The box is on a par with what other guests will receive. This is my private gift to you: my pledge.' He added with that gentle regard for her comfort that attended all he said: 'My sister joins me in offering it to you.'

She saw at once that it was unique, and of considerable value. 'A Russian trinket,' he explained, 'such as they exchange as Easter gifts.' An egg-shell in gold and enamel, exquisitely worked. 'But inside it again,' he said, 'is the token of our understanding.'

Two tiny hands clasped, in palest coral, with cuffs of the tiniest alternate diamonds and pearls. Her first, almost shocked, reaction was to say: 'It's far, far too valuable, indeed it is!'

'Its value is in its promise; that's all,' he said. 'You could not refuse it!'

Its promise. That never again, though times and conditions might change—need she ever feel utterly friendless: utterly alone. 'No,' she said, almost humbly. 'I couldn't refuse it; and with all my grateful heart I will just say thank you; and that, with or without this exquisite outward sign—I shall never forget. I shall never, never forget.'

Sir Frederick had been fortunate in his beautiful evening weather. Next day it rained.

Dorabella came to their sitting-room. 'I am going down to the boudoir, Miss Dove, to say a word to Mama.'

'Then I'll go to my room, I think, for a little while. We were so late last night. Will you knock when you come upstairs again?'

'Yes, have a rest!' She waited while Jane came with her down the corridor to her own bedroom, smiled at her, closed the door softly and went away. Jane curled up in her easy chair, opened the china box to a tinkle of music, took out the enamelled egg: and with the two tiny clasped hands in the palm of her own hand, sat dreaming...

Sat dreaming; awakened sharply from her dream. A phrase, unbidden, started up in her mind, heard but not noted, lying all this time beneath the level of her consciousness. 'I am going down to the boudoir—to say a word to Mama.'

To say a word...

All too typical of Dorabella's ingenious little fibs. I did not say I would *stay* with Mama, Miss Dove. I spoke the exact truth. I said I would speak a word to her. And so I did. And then...

And then?

How much Dorabella contrived to see of Richard Havering in these days, it had been difficult to guess; brief mysterious absences, accounted for by just such clever little evasions; meetings, supposedly accidental, out riding or while he was working on the tapestry. And now...

She has made an assignation, thought Jane. Last night at Sir Frederick's party, they were together; she has made an assignation to meet him again today. It was horrible to her to interfere; to seem to intrude her own personality

—but part of her duty was to protect her charge from this particular folly, or what was judged by her elders to be a folly (and indeed—what else?)—and she must be true to her bond. She ran to the cupboard, took out her cloak; slipped out into the corridor. As she passed Lady Mellowes' bedroom, Bates, the maid, came out with a finger to her lips: my lady was sleeping, tired from last night's late evening party. Jane nodded, all her fears confirmed: and sped on.

From within the dining-room—no sound. She tapped at last—no answer. With a beating heart, she went in. Nobody there. She searched through the hot-house, full of its luxuriant palms, any place where two lovers might go to be for a little while alone; sick with herself and her duty, yet resolutely pursuing it. No sign. The rain was falling lightly; she drew up the hood of her cloak and stepped out on to the terrace. There was a gazebo set on a little artificial eminence, surrounded by lily ponds. Careful to make no secret of her approach, calling Dorabella's name—now that she was no longer within earshot of the house—she made her way to it. No lovers there. She crossed to a great oak whose heavy branches might have sheltered them from the light rain. Still no one . . .

At this point, Lord Brunel's disputed land marched with that of the Dower House. She saw him riding slowly by; he changed course, rode up to her, dismounted and saluted her, standing holding his horse with a hand close up against the bit. 'Miss Bird! How agreeable to meet with you! But do you walk all alone—and in the rain?'

'I don't mind it,' she said, evading other issues. 'Such gentle rain as this is a sort of—refreshment.'

'And something of a refreshment, perhaps, to walk alone?'

'To walk alone?' she echoed, surprised.

'Miss Arabella Mellowes is a charming young lady, no doubt; but Miss Bird has, I think, a mind somewhat beyond that of a pretty little, spoilt little girl full of self-centred chatter. Do you not sometimes long to stretch it in a conversation more worthy of its powers?'

She was astonished: confused, at a loss. That he should so condescend to converse with her!—who appeared too haughty to do so with those so far her superiors ... And speak of her as he did ... And above all, speak so of the very same young lady whose cause she was supposed to promote with him ... She said: 'Indeed, it's not through any such preference that I walk alone.'

'Then you won't object if I walk a little way *with* you?'

'My lord, if you will excuse me—I am in fact just returning to the house; and in a little haste.'

'Well, then I will hasten with you so far; and for an excuse, may call in and pay my respects.'

'Lady Mellowes is, I know, resting after last night's party.'

'Then we'll part at the drive and I'll go my way, not disturbing her.'

And he walked with her, the rein over his arm, she hurrying her steps; he pleasantly chatting. No sign now of stiffness or pride. They spoke of the famous accident, she praised Dorabella's riding, trying manfully to bring the conversation back to the perfections of that young lady. But he would have none of it. 'Miss Mellowes is a spoilt little miss, without one half of your brains or personality—and you know it!'

'My lord—you mock me! What can you know of my brains or personality?—or indeed of hers?'

'Very little of yours, since I am permitted to see so little of you. But I have seen something of *her*; and if you have not at least twice the intelligence and ability, I despair of womankind.'

'You wrong her. She is full of excellencies. She is, of course, still a very young girl—'

'Very well; then let us say that I don't think I really care a great deal for very young girls.'

'Young girls grow up,' she suggested with some temerity, 'and become older girls.'

'If I thought this young girl might grow up to be an older one with half the character of her *institutrice*,' he said, using the French word as perhaps the more delicate way of referring to her own position in the household, 'I should not quite despair of her!' But, seeing her look of confusion and distress, he relented. 'Well, I must tease you no more. You are not used enough, I fear, to compliments which the much less worthy Miss Adorabella complacently accepts as her due.' And he stopped in the gravelled driveway, smiled down at her from his great height, lifted his tall riding hat and mounted and rode away. She entered through a side door, took off the damp cloak and went, almost stunned with bewilderment, up to her room.

Miss Ferris was standing there. She said: 'Where have you been?'

Jane was taken aback. 'I've been ... Out walking. For a short walk.'

'You have been out walking—in the rain—alone?'

'I went out alone,' said Jane, telling a half-truth; but not willing to speak, without first some consideration, of that talk with Lord Brunel.

'Where is Arabella?'

'What business is that of yours?' thought Jane; 'I am not responsible to *you*.' She said: 'I understood that she was going to her mother.'

'She is not with her mother, as I think you are well aware. So where is she?'

'I don't know, Miss Ferris,' said Jane.

'Is it not your business to know?'

'Surely not every moment of every hour of the day?'

'What else are you here for?'

Jane's temper began to rise. 'If Miss Mellowes declares her intention of going to her mother's room—am I to march her there under guard? I accepted what she said and snatched a few minutes of freedom for myself.'

'Are you duties so arduous that you need evade them for what you describe as a few minutes of freedom?'

'I have no complaint to make as to my duties,' said Jane, angrily. 'And with respect, ma'am, if I had, I should not address them to you, but go direct to Lady Mellowes.'

'I run this household. It was I who engaged you.'

'Then it is you who may accept my notice. I will not be spoken to in such a tone as this.' She had stood all this time, unmoving. Now she flung the damp cloak down on to the bed. 'The moment Lady Mellowes is free, I will tell her of what has occurred.'

'Will you tell her also that you in fact spent your "few minutes of freedom" in sneaking out to an assignation with none other than Lord Brunel?'

'I met Lord Brunel by accident. He walked back with me some of the way to the house.'

'By accident? Shielded by the branches of the oak, down beyond the gazebo—from which you came creeping out furtively and hurrying homewards—'

Jane heard her no further. 'What do you mean by that? What do you mean by "furtively", what do you mean by "an assignation", and "shielded by the branches of the oak"? What *can* you mean?'

Miss Ferris shrugged insolently. 'I think you know very well indeed what I must mean.'

They faced one another: the tall, handsome woman with her fine, curving bosom and hips, in her well-cut dark dress; the slender figure in its quiet grey. Both were white faced, in both anger grew to a point almost beyond control. 'How dare you?' cried Jane. 'How dare you make such suggestions to me?'

'What suggestion did Lord Brunel make to you, I should like to know? Or had the suggestion been made long ago and was now, in that hiding place, being put into performance; not for the first time, I dare say ...' And as Jane stood transfixed, speechless: 'Oh, don't imagine,' said Miss Ferris, 'that I have not watched you all this time, at your work! A husband catcher; or, failing that, the ensnarement of a rich protector: I know your kind! First ogling at that fortune-hunting creature and when he would have none of you—much chance a penniless governess would have with *him*!—transferring your attentions to another, to the heir, the very heir of this noble house—'

She stammered: 'Do you mean...? Are you referring to...?'

'I refer to Mr. Dominic Mellowes, as well you know. Will you deny that he has swerved in his fidelity to his cousin—?'

Dominic dancing with her at the ball; so friendly, just a little flirtatious ... She recalled that she had glanced over rather anxiously lest Adorabella grow jealous. Dominic asking her if she would not be happy to be mistress of such a home and estate as his; her laughing answer: 'Are you making me an offer?' ... She said stiffly: 'Mr. Mellowes has paid me some very trifling attentions—with the object, as I have always been well aware, of making his cousin jealous and so turning more of *her* attention to himself.'

'And no better object could he have found for his "trifling attentions" ... Ogling, languishing: oh, I've heard of your conduct that night at the ball they were so misguided as to take you to. A very Marquis, forsooth! —in his cups, I daresay, as he usually is. But his Mama soon saw you off that pitch, did she not, my dear?'

'In fact she invited me to her masked ball soon afterwards.'

'Or he forged an invitation—which no doubt might account for the masks. Rapscallion as he is—a fine prétendu, I must say, noble or otherwise!'

'It has all been a joke: a joke on every side. That and everything else; it's all been just an innocent nonsense.'

'Nonsense, indeed? The "two proposals", the "one very

positive offer"? I know what kind of offer that will have been, if nobody else does. Why even....' She grew if possible a shade more white and even in her own sick, cold rage, Jane could perceive the subtle change of tone. 'Even the poor tutor, chased after, pursued, to pander for your greed for admiration, your flagrant husband hunting.'

'Ah, yes,' said Jane, bursting out with it savagely. 'There we have it, don't we? A kind word from the tutor—' But again Miss Ferris over-rode her. 'And now it's Brunel! Feigning indifference, feigning a wish not to be introduced into his presence.... But you had been introduced into his presence, hadn't you? And soon found the means to follow it up, sneaking out to who knows how many secret assignations as I observed today? Buttering him up, regaling him, no doubt, with false stories about this family, this whole household—what else should account for his continued reserve? Betraying confidences reposed in you, most foolishly, I have always considered, a mere servant in this house as you are—'

'As I was,' said Jane. 'I will be one no longer. I have harmed no one, betrayed no one, behaved with entire propriety; there has been none other to find fault with me—'

'None other? Why, your own pupil—'

'A young girl, a child; piqued at receiving less than her mead of admiration—and even that done deliberately by her cousin in an attempt to cause her jealousy—do you suppose I was not aware of it? But never mind all that. Innocent or guilty, it makes no difference. I'll stay no longer under one roof with such a woman as you. Small and humble I may be: but I can look down from a height, Madam, that you will never know; and find you—contemptible.' She formed a resolution and this time knew that it must be so. 'I will leave this house today.'

Miss Ferris said, cold as death: 'You will leave when the officers of the law permit it.' And as Jane stood, incredulous, she grabbed up the pretty things still lying on the little table. 'These are valuable objects. They do not belong with a governess. Where did you get them?'

Jane, white with fury, tried vainly to snatch back the tiny coral hands, the enamelled Easter eggs. 'Give them to me! They're mine.'

'Since when? Since you went last night to Robin's Grange. Such treasures lie about everywhere there, I'm told.'

'Dear God! Do you accuse me—?'

'I ask you one question. Were these things in your possession when you came to the Dower House? No, they were not. You came by them last night, at Sir Frederick Travenne's.'

Jane stood confounded into silence. She stammered out at last: 'Everyone there was given a present.'

'And the governess was given these presents? Others received a pretty trinket, a china figure, a golden thimble —Lady Mellowes, I know, had an ivory fan. But Miss Bird, governess, gets a hundred, two hundred, pounds' worth of gifts! Find them, no doubt, tied with ribbons to a bough?—a charming little party present from Sir Frederick Travenne; consumed with love for her, like all the rest.'

'Yes,' said Jane. 'Since you ask me—he did give them to me.' And she cried out suddenly, almost screaming in the sick depths of her bitterly resentful rage: 'Gave them to me. To me, the lowliest of the low, the poor creeping thing that you think me, that you had almost made of me, indeed, until he raised me up, until he told me that I was—that I was worthy of his friendship and his— kindness; and gave me these two clasped hands in token of what he said...'

Miss Ferris stood staring at her; with one hand picked up the pretty things from the palm of the other and, as though she shed filth, dropped them back on to the table where they had lain. 'I believe you,' she said. 'Such a creature as that, no doubt, must pay pretty handsomely to satisfy his desires...'

Jane lifted her hand and with three hard, vicious swipes, hit out across the handsome face, and hit again and hit again; and taking the reeling woman by the shoulders, thrust her out of the room and slammed the door after her.

Chapter 9

If Bates knocked at the door, she did not hear it; knew only that the maid had entered and was standing at the bedside. She said in her quiet, unemotional way: 'Well, Miss—it seems to be my turn again!' and turned away, returning in a moment with a sponge dipped in cold water. 'Come, sit up, Miss, let me bathe your poor face; it will calm you.' And she raised the sobbing girl, held her against her own hard, bony shoulder, pressed the cold sponge against her throbbing temples, her burning cheeks. 'Be quiet, Miss, be calm, you'll make yourself ill . . .' She went again to the basin, came back with the cold water renewed. 'There, there—be quiet: be calm . . . !'

The level voice soothed her, she fought for control, the terrible sobbing ceased. She leant her weary forehead against that hard, supporting arm. 'Please help me! Please help me! I don't know . . . I can't think . . . I don't know what I must do.'

'Just be calm, Miss; quiet and calm . . .' But after a while, she said: 'You are to come down with me, Miss, as soon as you are ready for it—and see her ladyship.'

'I won't see anyone, Bates. I just want to go away.'

'That won't be possible yet, Miss . . .'

Jane clutched at her, terrified. 'What do you mean?'

'Only that her ladyship must see you first, Miss Bird,' said Bates, quietly and reasonably. She half lifted the girl from the bed, led her to the dressing-table, forced her down on to the chair before it. 'We have been here before, Miss, haven't we? Do you recall how my lady sent me up to brush your hair ... ?'

The brush went rhythmically through the long, soft locks; the even voice talked on. 'Miss Arabella is up at the Great House; Mr. Callie came down to tell us. She found her mother asleep it seems, and, wishing to give you an hour of rest, you being tired from the great party last night, decided to go on up to the House and enquire for some horse that it seems has gone lame. She's a great one for the horses, is Miss Arabella; and quite a little authority, so they say. Well, and then Sir Dermot found her there having a cup of tea with her ladyship, and was telling her of some great mystery relating to the tapestry that they've been puzzling over ever so long, a small line of black stitches; and Miss Arabella, it seems, solved it all in a moment, "Why, Uncle," she says, "that must mean a bar sinister," she says; and though I don't know what that means, Miss, it appears that everyone else does; and there's great excitement and discussion going on at the Great House, everyone knowing now what it means, but not even Miss Arabella able to tell them what it implies ... And then it appears that a great event occurred, for Sir Dermot met with his lordship, Lord Brunel, riding across the water-meadows and prevailed with him to come up to the House to call upon her ladyship; and you can guess, Miss, whether Miss Dorabella was not taken to the drawing-room and is still there according to Mr. Callie— and his lordship very affable and friendly ...' She put down the brush and smiled at the reflection in the glass. 'And whatever it all may or may not mean, Miss, it's proved quite a blessing to you and me!—for in the telling your tears are dry and your face is calm again and your hair combed and arranged—and you will go down now, very quiet and cool, to where her ladyship waits for you ...'

'Yes,' said Jane. 'You're right. I had better go.' And she took the thin, dry hand and held it a moment against her cheek. 'You have been a very kind friend to me,' she said. 'I shall always remember it.'

Lady Mellowes sat in her own chair in the drawing-room —that lovely room of white and gold, where first Jane had seen her, sitting so sweet and smiling, the little Dowager, with her gesture of outstretched, welcoming white hands. She was not smiling now; her face was very pale, as Jane had never seen it before; very strained and sad.

Turned away from her, her face buried in her hands, stood Hannah Ferris; and Callie was perched on the edge of a chair between them. He rose when Jane entered and came and took her hand and led her forward. He said: 'Well—she has come.'

Neither woman moved. Jane said: 'I came because you sent for me, my lady. Then I will go and never in all my life set foot in this house again.'

'Certain accusations have been made,' said Lady Mellowes. 'Before we agree to part—let me hear your side of it all.'

'There is no question of agreement, my lady. If you had heard how I was spoken to, you would know that whatever may happen, I shall go.'

'Very well; sit down—'

'I prefer to stand, my lady.'

'Very well,' said Lady Mellowes again.

'I'll be brief, my lady, if I can. Time's passing and I leave this house tonight. I came here to Robinsford,' said Jane, standing there, swaying a little in her exhaustion yet resolute not to give way again to weakness or tears, 'thinking to myself that I came into servitude. I found only kindness and graciousness, my lady, for which I thank you for ever; and no hint of my inferior position —except only from one. You took me among your family; they spoke with me on terms of equality—perhaps I too easily accepted and responded. You took me into company—I made no secret of my position, but there too I was met with the kindness of an equality—and once again, perhaps I accepted it too easily. And yet,' she said, almost piteously, 'how could I not respond? Was I to be "missish" as Callie called me?' But she pulled herself together. 'And then through an accident, I made the acquaintance—the barest acquaintance—of Lord Brunel.

'All this, my lady, has been turned against me; that I have—ogled and languished were the words used—at the gentlemen to try to find myself a husband or a rich protector. I make no protest, my lady; I simply tell you what has been said to me. As to Lord Brunel—I spoke with him at the time of the accident and in your presence on the two later occasions when he called to enquire if I was better. Never other than that, have I exchanged one word with him. Today, he overtook me while he rode in the park; dismounted and walked a little way with me, intending to call here; but, on my telling him that your ladyship was resting, he would not trouble you, and so he left me. I was in the park alone because I had found Miss Mellowes to be missing, and was out searching for her; for no other reason. What has been made of that meeting with Lord Brunel, my lady, I won't repeat— because I hope that for all my humble situation here, I am more of a true lady than she who could say such things. And for the rest . . .'

'Callie,' said Lady Mellowes quietly, 'bring a chair, if you please. Miss Dove, you must sit down; you're not well enough to go on standing there.'

Jane sat; but she said with cold disdain: 'My name, my lady, is Miss Bird.'

A flush of pink mounted up into the pale cheeks; died down again. 'Well—I understand how you must feel, to speak so to me. So—please continue, Miss Bird.'

'The rest you will not believe, my lady, I suppose. At Miss Baines' ball, I made the acquaintance of Sir Frederick Travenne. He, who also suffers what he calls "an irrational humility" understood something—understood all—of what I felt that night. We spent some little time together —the length of the supper dance—and became in that time, understanding friends. He became, at any rate, a friend to me. He said to me then that if ever I were in need, I should turn to him...' She said with angry scorn: 'Another construction, of course, has been placed upon that.'

Lady Mellowes only looked down at the white hands folded in her lap. 'Let us continue to the end.'

'It was for this reason—because I felt him so truly my friend—that I accepted his invitation for last night's party; though, as you well know, my lady, I had avoided all others. And there he spoke to me again, in the same fashion; and renewed his offer of—help—if ever I should need it. Perhaps,' said Jane, 'I should put that offer in its right perspective. His words were that now and for the future, however much conditions might have changed, if ever I should need it—I should still find help and a refuge with him. With him and with his sister,' she added deliberately. 'For this reason he introduced me to her.'

'And the gifts? You showed us only a musical box.'

'He didn't wish to embarrass me; I had a gift, in tune with all the other gifts, to be shown publicly. But this other gift was to be between us: between him and me— and Lady Fielding, his sister. A private gift: not to be shown round.' She rose from the chair and stood very erect and still. She said: 'I have done only one thing throughout all this, my lady, for which I feel the smallest need to be ashamed. It was uncontrolled and utterly unwomanly to hit another woman across the face; my excuse is that she had poured the venom of her filthy mind over even that gift—of his kindness.' And she quoted it, viciously: 'I suppose that such a creature as that must pay handsomely for the satisfaction of his desires...'

Lady Mellowes seemed to shrink in her chair into a small, pale, trembling heap, her white hands up to her face. She cried out: 'Oh! Oh *no!*' But Callie got up quietly and went to Miss Ferris and put his arm around her shoulders and Jane saw, suddenly that she was weeping. 'Oh, Hannah!' he said. 'This bitter, bitter tongue of yours...!'

Hannah Ferris turned in the curve of his arm. She lifted to Jane a face stained with tears. She mumbled: 'I'm sorry. I apologise...'

Jane took not the smallest notice. She said to Lady Mellowes: 'Now—may I ask if the law has been sent for? Or am I free to go?'

Lady Mellowes dropped her hands from her face. She said in a small, sad voice: 'Must you go?'

'That such things should ever be said of your lady-ship, is, of course, unthinkable. But I am a woman no less than yourself; and was once a lady. I have not after all always been a servant; I have known some little wealth and comfort and a happy home. And they have been said of me. So I am going.'

'But...' The sweet face turned this way and that. 'Where can you go to, my child?'

She longed to ask advice; but no doubt advice would come, in its own form. 'Only one home is open to me,' said Jane. 'I had better go there.'

'You mean go to Sir Frederick?'

'All that holds me back is the thought that there may be other minds like—hers.'

'I have begged your pardon,' said Hannah Ferris, sullenly. 'I have apologised. I retract it all.'

Again Jane ignored her totally. 'I am thinking of Sir Frederick's reputation, my lady; mine, obviously enough, is of very little consequence.'

'You can't go there, my dear girl; kind though they may be, they are strangers.'

'And to go from this house—' began Miss Ferris.

Now Jane did address her: 'Ah, indeed—from this house! Something scandalous might be said about this house; and that would be a pity, wouldn't it?—though so much vilification may go on as to others. It might even be said that I had fled this house because of the unkindness I received here.'

Miss Ferris stood with bowed head. Callie said: 'You are ungenerous, Miss Dove—'

'Miss Bird,' corrected Jane, rigidly.

'Then shall I say that Miss Bird is ungenerous; as I think Miss Dove would not be. You were christened that, out of much affection,' said Callie, gently. 'Will you not be as good and sweet as we knew you to be, when we gave you that name?'

'Why, Callie—why Mr. Carrell—take good care! You too are on the list of my attempted conquests: "the poor tutor" who was to be good enough to pander to my craving for compliments.'

'That was ungenerous in you, Hannah,' said Callie, in his own, always half-teasing, kindly way. 'If—having rejected it for all these years—you should begrudge my poor, despised devotion to another.'

She raised her proud head. 'I have not despised you. You know that it has been—otherwise. But I represent a noble family. It is not for me to—to ally myself with—'

'With a poor tutor. Well—that has been your conviction, my dear, and to my mind, poor tutor though I be, it has been one of false values. It has made a bitter woman of you, I have watched it through the years: a bitter and jealous woman—who at heart are far better and nobler than you have allowed yourself to be. And I mean that word not in the sense of family nobility. For...' His hand reached into a pocket. He said, quietly: 'For to that, my dear, it now seems—you have no claim.'

'No *claim*?'

He said; 'The mark in the tapestry, proves now to be intended to represent a bar sinister. And, Hannah—it is against your branch of the family. Sir Dermot will explain it to you when you ask it of him; but the fact is that you and yours, far back to that little line of black—have had no legitimate right to the family name.'

She stood absolutely rigid; beneath the red tear-stains her face was an ashen grey. Lady Mellowes said, in pity: 'Oh, Callie—need you have told her now?'

'Yes,' he said. 'This was the very time to tell her. Now when in her pride she has so deeply injured this poor girl; now when she can at last feel free to put her hand in mine and say, "Callie, I am yours; look after me!"' And he went to her and took her hand. 'Hannah,' he said, 'you have something to say to Miss Bird.'

She did not take away her hand; but stood for a long time, with her head bent, considering. She said at last: 'Yes. I was wrong, Miss Bird—utterly wrong. Whatever I may be, whatever I may have believed myself to be—I was wrong to speak to you as I did; to speak so to anyone. I have been—perhaps I have been bitter and jealous, as he says; I have loved, and thought myself obliged to forego my love—I have watched with envy the conquests of other women over the hearts of men.' She did not look at Callie. 'Perhaps over *his*. It has been my fault; but perhaps you will a little pity me, rather than blame. Either way, I was deeply at fault, and I acknowledge it to you. I lost my head at last, lost my temper, lost all womanliness. You struck me—and I will acknowledge that you were justified in doing so. I beg your pardon; and I beg the pardon of all those whom I slandered, in slandering *you*.' She was silent; and as Jane too stood silent, she said: 'I think there is no more, that I can offer.'

'I think so too,' said Callie. He said: 'Miss Dove—?'

She gave way. 'Very well. I must accept such an apology. No one could refuse it. But ... To accept is easy perhaps, it's a matter of words. But to forgive ...'

'Miss Dove!' said Callie again, on a different note.

'Very well, I'll say that I forgive, I'll do my best to forgive. But as for forgetting, that is out of my power. So, my lady,' said Jane, now addressing Lady Mellowes, 'allow me to go, and at once, for I feel that I shall stifle if I don't get away from this house. I will leave my things; Miss Bates, I know, will pack and forward them for me. I'll take only what I need; and so go away.' And she cried, brought suddenly almost to the edge of hysteria: 'You *must* see that I must get away ... !'

'But where to, my dear child—where to?' Lady Mellowes suggested diffidently: 'To the Great House?—just till arrangements can be made for you—?'

'I will leave this place and this family. I must go.'

'But to Sir Frederick's ...'

'Lady Fielding is there,' said Callie, doubtfully.

'And I shall go to her,' said Jane. 'He will explain it all.' She turned to leave the room: 'I will pack a few things; if your ladyship would be so good as to arrange a cab for me ... ? I will call in and say goodbye to you, as I pass through the hall.'

As I pass through the hall: through the high, lofty, beautiful hall that has been the centre of this loving and lovely house—which now I leave for ever ...

She knew they must be continuing to discuss it, as she arranged her things, swiftly, leaving neatly folded bundles on the bed for Bates to pack into her trunk and send on. Her cloak was still damp—was it so short a time ago that she had slipped out, never dreaming that it was for the last time?—except on her final departure. Carrying the small basket case, she went down the great curve of the staircase, came to the hall: tapped at the drawing-room door: went in.

Callie was not there, nor Hannah Ferris. But Bates was there, with Payne, Dorabella's maid, standing with humble, folded hands and head bent before her ladyship. 'Oh, my lady, I don't know if I did right?'

'Yes, yes, Payne. Of course, and I thank you for it.' As the door opened, Lady Mellowes turned to Jane a face far whiter and more strained even than it had been before. 'Oh, Miss Dove!—come and help me, please, please help me!—what am I to do?'

All memory of the scene just passed seemed to have gone; if she looked with a sort of vague wonder at Jane's cloak and bonnet, she hardly saw them, her mind was so far away. 'Payne—explain to Miss Bird.'

'It was the letters, Miss,' said Payne. 'In Miss Arabella's waste-basket. She sat so long scribbling; and when she had left the room, I went to clear up, just as usual, and there was the basket full of crumpled-up notes, tossed aside, some not even falling in but just littering the floor. And—and...' Her face began to crumple.

'Come, Payne, her ladyship has told you you did nothing wrong,' said Bates, severely. 'The fact is, Miss Bird, that Payne could not help but see some of the words in Miss Dorabella's big hand. And such words they were that she thought it right to examine the papers no more but to bring them all to me; and I, having heard what she had to say, have brought them to her ladyship.'

Lady Mellowes bent her head and seemed almost to sway where she sat. 'They are notes to Mr. Havering, Miss Dove,' she said. 'She is planning to meet him tonight— and elope with him.'

'To elope!' cried Jane. 'To elope with Mr. Havering?'

'I've thought it right to read through the letters now. Each is an attempt at outlining some plan—different plans, different instructions as to the same plan...' She put out her hand and caught at Jane's. 'Help me! Don't desert me now!'

'Where is Miss Ferris?' said Jane across her head, to Bates.

'Gone to her room, Miss, with a sick headache. She is prostrated, Miss, I think she could be of no assistance just now. And Mr. Carrell has gone back to the Great House. You will see, Miss,' said Bates in her own quiet way, 'that but for you, her ladyship is alone.'

'Yes.' She took off her bonnet, undid the clasp of her cloak, knelt down by Lady Mellowes' chair. It was her turn now. She said: 'Bates will get us each a glass of wine, my lady, with your permission—and we'll think what best to do.'

'Yes, Miss,' said Bates. She went out of the room, returned with a tray bearing glasses. 'You won't want Payne and me, my lady. Of course we shall be ready if you ring for us.'

Jane took her glass and with a glance for permission, sat down in the chair close to Lady Mellowes'. 'Don't despair, my lady; we'll find a way out. But explain to me first—what is her actual plan?'

'Oh, my dear, who can tell? Each note—most of them half finished—(and can you imagine the indiscretion of the child!—leaving them all just crumpled-up for all the world to see)—each suggests some different arrangement. It does seem that a carriage has been arranged for, not one of our own; and this is to be at that place or this place, at that time or this time—but at any rate, somewhere this evening, and after dark. She will meet him there and go with him—go with him...' For a moment she broke down. 'He appears to have some private menage in Robinstown!'

'Dear God! It's true that he has a little house in—in Capsicum Street. But surely she won't go there alone with him—and unmarried...?'

'What else is an elopement, my dear?'

'I suppose she despairs of your permission?'

'Permission to marry such a man! What can he be, Miss Dove?—to agree to such a plan, with this young, foolish, wilful little girl, taking advantage of her inexperience ... To her it's all romance and nonsense; galloping hooves carrying them through the moonlight, wrapped in their cloaks—the dominoes, if you please!—they are to wear the dominoes from the masked ball at Lord Chalmers'— you remember it?'

'I remember not going to it,' said Jane, a trifle bitterly;

but she fought her own feelings down. 'Is it not simplest, my lady, just to send a message to the Great House, informing them of the plan and asking them to deal with Mr. Havering; while you speak to Dorabella here? Where *is* Dorabella, by the way?'

'Still up at the House; and safe, I suppose, for nothing is planned till after dark. She may well be glad of the excuse not to have to face me—her mother—with such plans already formed in her head for my deception, knowing what pain it must cause me.'

'No doubt it was for a chance to pass him this note, making final arrangements, that she went there in the first place?'

'I suppose so. And of course now, as you say,' said Lady Mellowes, 'I suppose it might be prevented. But only for the moment. Sir Dermot may dismiss Mr. Havering, of course he'll do so; but there's nothing to stop his remaining in Robinstown; and with this poor, infatuated girl—'

Not the only poor infatuated girl! For here, indeed, was an end to dreams!—and an end not brought about by her own action, but beyond her control entirely. Nor could her respect endure for a man who, as Lady Mellowes had said, would so take advantage of an innocent, trusting young creature, whose only real charm for him—and one could not blink it—must be the availability of her fortune. Other girls might be richer; but this girl, it seemed, was available and immediately so. That Richard Havering genuinely loved her, Jane could not bring herself to believe. He danced with her, flirted with her, kissed her wrist in that small, secret way of theirs; but these letters ... 'Do you not think, my lady, that the notes seem— well, seem largely promoted by Dorabella herself? Is it not usually the man who makes the assignation, arranges the plan ...?'

'It may be so; but he, you see, apparently agrees. And what will they say at the Great House?' said Lady Mellowes, almost trembling, 'at this end to their dreams of a union with the Brunel lands?'

Jane hesitated. 'If your ladyship won't misunderstand me—and I have today been sufficiently misunderstood, I think, to warrant some hesitation—I think that that dream had no existence and never could have, outside Dorabella's own family. Lord Brunel told me today that he—well, he finds her too young and—and childish, I think, my lady—to be of any interest to him.' She added quickly that she had tried to suggest to him that even young girls grew up; but did not add his lordship's expression of doubt that this particular young girl would ever grow up in a way to suit his inclination. 'To be blunt, my lady, I believe that—Mr. Havering or no Mr. Havering—Adorabella would have no chance with Lord Brunel; no chance at all.'

'Oh, well...' Lady Mellowes sighed. 'There will be great repinings up on the hill; but at least we shall hear no more of glass eyes and wooden legs.' If indeed, she added wretchedly, they heard any more of Dorabella herself. 'But this must somehow be stopped. What are we to do?' (If only that foolish girl would have taken her cousin! —who for so long had adored her, would make her so admirable a husband, knowing all her faults and follies and yet loving her throughout!)

'I have sometimes fancied ... Everything,' said Jane, 'has been so tainted by those things that have been said to me but an hour ago, that I find it hard to speak out. But I will say again, boldly, my lady, that I have sometimes fancied that she resented Mr. Dominic's apparent attentions to me; that she was jealous—as he had intended that she should be.'

'All these too-easy admirers have spoilt her. She can no longer brook any other girl's receiving attentions.'

Jane thought it over. 'I think there you a little wrong her, my lady, if I may say so. I have seen her delighted that some other girl—and a pretty girl, too—should seem to be flattered and courted: at the Baines ball, for example. Dorabella isn't greedy; she has no reason to be.'

'You mean then, that if she is jealous it suggests that, whether she knows it or not, she at least a little loves her cousin?' She sighed again. 'If only it were he that she were planning to elope with! But poor Dommie—do you see him in an aura of moonlight and domino cloaks and galloping hooves . . . ?'

'Domino cloaks!' said Jane.

'Yes, I told you, that's what—'

'And masks?'

She was not slow, the little Dowager. 'Miss Dove—what is it that you mean to suggest?'

'Her cousin Dominic—with a coach; cloaked and masked . . . Hastening up to the meeting place; with whispers enjoining silence, seizing her by the arm, carrying her off to the waiting coach . . . And a driver instructed not to stop, whatever the pleas from within . . .'

'*If* there were pleas from within?'

'Cloaked and masked—galloping through the moonlit night with a clatter of hooves on the road; and a young man with his arms around her—whom I think in her secret heart she at least a little bit loves . . .'

Lady Mellowes was sitting bolt upright now, the pale face flushed, eyes shining . . . 'If she were but to choose *him*! What happiness through all the family—what happiness for her, fortunate girl, her whole life through! He is the very salt of the earth.' She clapped her little hands. 'It would compensate them even for the loss of Lord Brunel, glass eye, wooden leg and all!' But the laughter faded. 'Nothing has been said about masks; only the dominoes.'

'He has but to arrive masked and she will be enchanted by it: the fun and the mystery—he may carry one for her, though of course for him there would be no mystery. But it would delight *her*.'

'But . . . If she is angry; if she won't love him after all . . . And even if she does—where shall they go?'

'He may tell the coachman to drive round and at last bring them back here.'

'She knows the roads too well. She will know they're not going to Robinstown ... And ... The other! Suppose he discovers what has happened and gives chase? Let her feel what she will for her cousin, if a second gallant comes dashing to the rescue, tears her from his arms, carries her off—double the romance of the original plan! And he'll do so. The moment he finds he's been tricked—what is to prevent him?'

I must leave this place, thought Jane; whatever comes of all this—today or tomorrow, I must leave this place and for ever; I couldn't continue here—too much has passed, I should never forget. And when I leave—I lose him for ever. So what matters it, how I lose him? Shall I not at least in the losing, do some good to these people who have been so good to *me*? And she said aloud, steadily: *'I* will prevent him.'

A second coach. A second set of masks and dominoes. A second game to be played. A second—elopement.

There were voices in the hall. The door flew open. 'Oh, Mama—I have brought you a visitor! But you will excuse me—I must fly upstairs, I have been all day at the Great House, I am exhausted...' A glimpse of silk petticoats, a shake of auburn curls, a bob curtsey, hastily sketched; 'Goodbye, my lord, and thank you for conducting me home,' and she was gone. And Lord Brunel stood uncertainly in the doorway. A footman, thrust aside by the impetuosity of his young mistress, announced awkwardly: 'My lord Brunel, to call upon her ladyship,' and, closing the door behind him, departed. Lord Brunel came forward.

Lady Mellowes stumbled to her feet and curtsied. Lord Brunel said sharply: 'You are unwell, Madam? I disturb you?'

'No, no, indeed. Pray sit down, my lord.' She resumed her own chair. 'It is so kind of you ... Do I understand that you have brought my daughter home from the Great House?'

He went down on one knee beside her. He said: 'You have been weeping!' And, as she did not reply, put his arms about her and said in a voice that shook: 'What is the matter, you break my heart with your tears. What has happened to distress you?'

She was utterly confounded. 'Lord Brunel—!'

He dropped his arms from about her. 'I beg your pardon. My feelings have carried me away. I had no right to—'

'Your feelings?'

'Surely you have known all this time that I have loved you?'

She could not comprehend it, she could not take it in. 'You have loved me? But you've been so—so cold, so—so proud with us...'

'Do you think I don't know that you all believe me guilty of stealing your land? Not a soul here has given me a smile—except this sweet thing, here, your daughter's companion. For the rest...'

She only repeated, dazed with it: 'You have loved me?'

'From the first moment. But how declare it?—among my enemies. Yet the land was mine; it came to me from my forebears, who acquired it in a manner that to all parties was perfectly honourable. Was I to—?'

'Never mind, what matters the land?' she said. 'You have *loved* me?'

He still knelt at her side. Now he put his arms back around her. 'And you—?'

She put her fair white arms about his neck, laid her cheek against his own to hide her blushes as though she were a young girl again, in her courting days. 'But of course, of course!' she said. 'I have loved you for ever.'

And so the famous Brunel acres would be brought back

into the Mellowes family again; and there would be rejoicing at the Great House as there was rejoicing here, for a different reason. But meanwhile ... 'My lady,' said Jane, at last, 'you will not have forgotten ... ?'

'Oh, no, and you're right to remind me. But now,' said Lady Mellowes, putting her white hand into her lover's close grasp, 'we have Lord Brunel to help us ...'

To the double elopement.

Dominic was sent for to come down hastily and in secret to the Dower House. Lord Brunel's carriage would be at their disposal and his coachman instructed. 'Best that *she* should use mine. *He* might recognise it as not that which was arranged for. Now we must examine these letters and be sure of the meeting place.' He pored over the crumpled papers. 'It's important that she leaves before he comes to the assignation. Some arrangement must be made—let Miss Bird perhaps send a message that she'll come to her room a little before the hour. She'll be afraid of getting delayed and will start off earlier. Have young Dominic waiting in my coach, as though Havering, too, came early; let him hustle her in, saying nothing, and the driver will whip up his horses. By the time the true lover arrives, the carriage will have departed and a second be waiting. We can't risk his finding her gone, galloping after them and spoiling everything.' He said to Jane: 'You will dissemble as long as you can? You are a brave girl, brave and loyal.'

'You're sure, Miss Dove, that you can go through with this?'

'Will he catch me in his arms when we come to the meeting place?' thought Jane, '—mistaking me for Adorabella? Will he take me in his arms and kiss me?' One kiss to last for all her lifetime—and that intended for another woman! She reflected guiltily that they would think a great deal less of her could they know that she went as much for her own sake as for Dorabella's: for love of a man, unworthy, untrustworthy and now proved

177

both: a fortune hunter, base seducer of a foolish innocent young girl, and for gain.... She thought of those other young girls, of the rich little, too often ill-favoured little, girls—all swooning over the attentions of one who looked beyond their plain faces to their fathers' money-bags: of a woman in Mayfair whose lover he had been—of the little, secret menage behind the painted yellow door in Capsicum Street. I must be as bad as he, she thought, if I can love him still; and knew that she did not, could not love him still, that this was something outside love, outside her own comprehension: a sick infatuation no less than Adorabella's—for a rogue, a villain who cared for her—penniless as she was—not one jot. And she thought rather wistfully of Adorabella, in the arms at this moment, little doubt of it, of the childhood love who had suffered in her young eyes only from being too familiar, too much available: of Lady Mellowes made happy, of Hannah Ferris permitting herself happiness at last. 'Only I,' she thought, 'am outside it all; bereft and alone.' She said steadily: 'I'll go through with it. I won't fail you.' (One moment in his arms—to last her a lifetime!)

'I am anxious, though,' said Lady Mellowes, to Brunel. 'What if he turns angry when he finds himself tricked? What if he takes her to—to that house—?'

'Young Mellowes will be there ahead of her,' he said, reassuringly, 'with your daughter. Even if she discovers her cousin's identity, if he fails in her love, even if he succeeds in it—she will somehow make her way to the place where this rogue was to take her. And even if she doesn't— we'll go there ourselves, and so rescue Miss Bird—and your daughter too, if she comes there ... I'll take my light phaeton, we'll make better time.'

All so hurried, so scrambled; ill thought-out, perhaps, but there was no more time. Dark was falling; already Dorabella would be making her secret preparations for flight; her maid, Payne, trembling yet loyally dissembling, had brought down a message—her young lady had the headache, was retiring to her bed, felt she should fall asleep at once, begged that nobody—*nobody*—would disturb her. Lady Mellowes said coolly: 'Tell Miss Arabella, Payne, that Miss Bird will open her door at nine o'clock and look in to see that she's no worse; but if she's sleeping, will not disturb her.' Nine o'clock was the hour of the assignation. And she smiled her own sweet smile at the anxious woman. 'All will yet be well, Payne; and so much of it thanks to you.' And, as the woman curtsied and went: 'And all will yet be well, indeed; and so very, very much thanks to our precious Miss Dove.'

'I'm not worthy,' said Jane, 'of such a word from you.' And knew it, alas! to be true.

Chapter 10

They watched, with fear and pity, the slight form, wrapped in the great black cloak, slipping, in supposed secrecy, out of the house; listened to hear the far rattle of carriage-wheels on the gravel—driving away. As the moment came up to nine, there was the sound of a coach again: and Lady Mellowes put her arms round Jane and kissed her. 'My good, brave, loyal little friend—now it is you!'

He was standing there waiting, by the door of the hired carriage as she crept to him through the shrubbery and into a far part of the driveway; both cloaked, she masked. She went into his arms. He kissed her lightly: held her lightly. For all my life time, she thought; this one kiss!— and gave herself up to him.

Now he held her fierce and close, his mouth was hard on hers. She thought, half swooning in his arms, that here lay all her joy: that if this must last her a lifetime, it would after all, be enough. But he relaxed his hold at last, hastened her into the coach. Not a word had been spoken, not a word was said as the carriage started into movement; again she was in his arms and his lips on hers. He leaned back in his corner at last, releasing her. He said: 'What?—masked and all?'

'Hush,' she said, whispering huskily to disguise her voice. 'The man will hear you.'

'What matter if he does?'

'I am frightened.'

'Will you not take off this mask?'

'Suppose someone should pass on the road...!' She repeated: 'I'm frightened.'

'To be riding off with your bold, bad lover! I can't help laughing,' he said, 'at the feelings of poor dear little Miss Dove, when she finds the made-up bolster in your bed.'

'It is hard on Miss Dove,' she suggested, murmuring.

'Oh, certainly! And I shall pay dear for this, if ever I meet her again. She has sweet, soft feathers, our little grey bird, but she pecks with a very hard beak.'

'When she is offended.'

'Which she is, very easily. She overheard me once, when I fought off three rascals that would have given her something to take offence at, indeed, in that chicken-skinned pride of hers. Two were merely enquiring as to fortune, and those I explained away to her; but the third had ambitions even less complimentary. I warned him that the young lady would prove "not amenable"; I believe now that she misheard it "not amiable"—she has never forgiven me since.' He laughed. 'Poor little dove!'

The moonlight flooded all the world outside with its brilliance; within the coach, it was darkly shadowed. He lounged back in his corner, her hand held lightly in his own. Did he feel how hers trembled?—how she started at that word 'amenable'? He had, after all, but defended her against insult and pain. And now he went on: 'Of course she has been taught in advance to disapprove. You were placed in her care for no reason but to guard her against me.'

She whispered the word: 'Fortune-hunter...'

'What a funny little creature you are!' he said. 'Crouching back in your corner (for all that your kisses are not the kisses, my pretty one, of a scared little miss: where did you learn so much?)—with your mask and your murmuring. The driver knows well enough what we are about;

or do you fear that the moonlight will peep in and see you, and shine out its alarm to a world not even dreaming as yet—let us hope!—that there's anything to be alarmed about? But as to fortune-hunting: well, my dear, I make no secret of it. My fortune must come through a woman—I have no other way of acquiring one. I have been something of a gambler, it's true. What little money I had I spent in placing myself in a position where such a woman might be found to provide for my future. How deny it?—and indeed why? Everyone else is only too ready to inform you of it.'

'Including those other young ladies who—whose fortunes you might have chosen?'

'What—a pipe out of you at last?' he said, laughing; for in her indignation at his cool cynicism, she had almost raised her voice. 'Are you jealous, then, my pretty, of those others?' He laughed again. 'Well, but the truth is that I have been much maligned. For to what other young ladies was I supposed to address myself? In the society your family has introduced me to—what *are* there but these wealthy young girls? I couldn't avoid them. Was I to attach myself only to the chaperones, to seize Mrs. Baines by the waist perhaps and jump about with her?— or with old Lady Cuff who really *has*, they say, under all those monstrous great skirts of hers, a wooden leg? Pretty girls, plain girls—I danced with them all, was civil to them all: was it my fault if they had this in common, that they all were rich? Was it my fault if they fell beneath the spell of my too-fatal charms? Was I to stand mute against a pillar with all the other wall-flowers?—did I do so, my hostess would soon have come bustling up with a sharp order to get back to work; I was not there to leave young ladies unpartnered. Much maligned! I tell you—I have been much maligned! Why, even the poor governess I favoured with a waltz—looked into her eyes, paid her some very pretty compliments as far as I recall; only she turned sour at the end and would have none of me. Did I enquire first of *her* fortune? I knew she had none.'

In her anguish, she withdrew her hand sharply from his. He caught at it again. 'Come—don't leave me! You can't be jealous because I confess to a kind word for poor Miss Dove. I did but dance with her and all the rest of them, as was required of me; was civil to them all.'

Plausible enough. True enough, probably to some extent; but not the whole truth ... With Miss Aurora Baines for one, he had not only danced and been civil. To carry herself over her own pain, she whispered that name.

'Ah, yes, Miss Baines. A nice girl, a dear girl, open and generous, (do you recall how she bought that gown and dressed up our poor little dove like an over-blown peacock?) and—well, it is hardly a secret, my dear, that she came all too frankly beneath the aforesaid spell. Nor were Mama and Papa too unwilling; they had no need to look for fortune or birth; darling Aurora's happiness was all to them. So—Miss Baines lay in wait for me, met me "accidentally"—not the only one to do that, my pet?— and Mama had a new lap-dog or Papa a new picture which would so much interest me—would I not come home with her and see ... ? Did I thereupon seize her immediately, money-bags and all? With her, I wouldn't even have had to elope. Or little Miss Feather, who'd have flown with me, all wings outspread?—or half a dozen others I could mention did not my innate sense of chivalry forbid. With far heavier money bags than yours, my pretty sweetheart. In my preference, do at least do yourself some justice. Have I not been true to you only?'

She faltered: 'I have heard of—of a lady in London—'

'Of a lady in London? Have you indeed? Well, I knew many ladies in London, but that was long, long ago, before I had the happiness to come to Robinstown and meet Miss Adorabella Mellowes. I can think of none, however, who could cause that enchantress much jealousy. I was young then and rather innocent—not the rake that you know me now; and fell into company that I didn't quite recognise to be what it was. When I did, I took refuge abroad. A certain lady—but you can hardly know of *her*—proved importunate and I made a somewhat scrambled departure.' He reached out to her. 'Is it not time for more kisses?'

Oh, love of my life!—your mouth on mine, so that my heart turns over in my breast; so that my arms must cling to you, my hands thrust themselves up hard against your fair head, drawing it down ever again, to my seeking lips ... Receiving these kisses, stolen from another woman! Hoarding up these moments that are not mine, to last me all my life...! He whispered, his mouth on hers: 'When we come to Capsicum Street...'

When they came to Capsicum Street—indeed, what then? What anger, what resentment, what cold rage?— what chill disgust at the memory of these kisses given— and received! But she could not forebear; her whole being was shaken with longing for him, she knew that her passion had awakened in his own cool, cynical desire, an answering fire. Let him be mine, she thought, at least till the end, till that terrible moment—when we come to Capsicum Street...

And they came. And though the yellow door stood closed there were lights in the house. He glanced out at them: said, coolly: 'Well—Callie is duly arrived. He is there to meet us.'

'*Callie?*'

'My nonsense girl! Do you think I would really rape you away from your home, destroy your innocence—in my passion for your gold? You have had your elopement and your moonlit drive and your kisses—though the kisses, I confess, rather more thorough than I intended: and now you'll go home with Callie and affairs may continue at a more conventional pace.'

'You weren't going to—? You wouldn't have—?'

'*Much* maligned!' he said, shaking his head, laughing. 'I told you—much maligned!' And the coach stopped and he opened the door and jumped out; and lifting her down, stood looking with those blue, blue, heaven-blue eyes, deep down into hers. 'Well—a very agreeable journey! Thank you, Miss Dove!'

She could only stand there; dumbfounded. He lifted away her mask, laughing down into her eyes. She stammered at last: 'You *knew*?'

'From the very first embrace. Do you think that so practised a rake couldn't tell one woman's kisses from another's?' And he turned to the opening of the yellow door. 'And here is our reception committee.'

Adorabella—clinging to her cousin's arm, half happy, half frightened. 'Oh, Richard—I have something that I must tell you...'

'And I have something that I must not tell *you*!' He smiled into Dominic's eyes. 'Well—a very pretty plot! And I see that it has worked. A thousand congratulations!'

'Richard! You don't *mind*?'

'You would have your elopement, Miss Adorable! What was I to do? Have I ever been able to resist you? You are much too much your own pet name, for one so weak as I. But to answer your question frankly—no, I don't mind. With all your witching ways and enchantments a man would be left with no will of his own at all. Your cousin is welcome to you!'

She paused—pouted—looked up at Dominic and burst into laughter; saw Jane and came to her. 'Oh, my darling Miss Dove,' cried Adorabella, drawing her into the narrow hallway, 'how good you have been and how happy it has made me! Dommie says that all this time it was I he cared for, he never even faltered for one moment, never even thought of you at all, except as—well, as—'

'As a decoy duck,' said Jane, summoning up her courage to smile at her. 'Yes, I know. I knew.'

'And poor Richard! It's too true, I have pursued him with my attentions, Dommie says it's been pitiful to watch me: forced him to assignations and romantic meetings, flirted with him till it would be uncivil—would have been unkind, Dommie says, and humiliating, not to have responded. I always thought him so surprisingly mild and milk-water; he was trying, I suppose, not to encourage me. But I . . . Poor Richard!'

'Oh, indeed,' said Richard, laughing, following them in, 'it has been all a great penance. I've suffered quite dreadfully.'

They moved to the door of the small sitting-room; within, everything was laughter and happiness. Jane caught sight of the tall figure of Lord Brunel with his love clinging, all smiles and happiness, to his arm. Callie was there with Hannah Ferris; that dark lock strayed, and Jane saw with what a proprietorial air he reached up his hand and smoothed it back against her head. Across the room, she smiled at Jane. Lady Mellowes was pushing her way through, coming up to her; taking her in her arms. 'My dear, is all well with you? You see there was nothing wrong in it after all: he had left a note for Callie, Callie rushed down to the house to tell us, just after you'd gone. We thought it best to come here by the more direct route, as fast as could be.'

'I am—quite all right,' said Jane, dully. 'He recognised me from the first. He knew it was a trick.'

'He is a noble fellow, after all: how good he has been about Adorabella! Lady Mellowes at the Great House, has always thought better of him than the rest of us have. But you! My good, brave girl! How much we shall owe to you always, even though, you see, no harm was intended.' But she looked into the bleak, white face. 'There was no trouble? He wasn't angry? No harm came to *you*?'

'No harm,' thought Jane. 'No harm. Only that I have exposed all my secret to him. Only that I have sat with him and let him mock me, cold-hearted as he is; knowing all along who it was that heard him. Only that he has used me for the release of his passions, recognising me for what I was...' And her secret heart was sick within her. 'Discovering me, even to myself as what I am...' She said: 'No harm, my lady. But it has been—a little exhausting. Permit me now to slip out quietly, and steal myself some fresh air. I will wait in the carriage until you are ready to leave...'

But Richard Havering was standing outside, in the corridor. He took her arm. 'Miss Dove—you think very ill of me?'

'If I do, then that must be mutual,' she said, drearily. 'Pray let me go now. I should like to be in the fresh air; and for a little while alone.'

He stood looking down at her as though undecided; jerked a thumb towards the crowded, noisy, happy room. 'You are the last of the diehards. You see how much everyone has now learned to love me! Only *you* resist.'

'Only I know all about you,' she said.

'I meant no harm to the child; and none came to her. Of course I had no intention of any foolish elopement.'

'Her money-bags were less heavy than those of the others; you said so—just now in the coach.' But at the mention of that drive, a blush suffused her pale face. She covered it over, saying hastily: 'Making a virtue of it, even then.'

'Addressing my virtues, however, towards yourself,' he suggested.

'Oh, yes—well...' It was all so confusing. 'To me or to others, you can make a virtue out of everything, I suppose. Even of bringing her—well bringing me, then, but you intended it for her, originally—to this house—'

'What's wrong with my house?' he asked, surprised. 'I kept it a secret. But I was entitled, I suppose, to a little privacy—away from all the good people at Robinsford.'

'I happen to know—if "all the good people at Robinsford" do not—who shared your privacy.'

He was silent a moment. Then: 'You've been eavesdropping again, Miss Dove,' he said.

'I overheard a man telling Callie. "A foreign woman, young and beautiful". Is it she who is to bring you your fortune? For in all this, you forget that you lately admitted to me that it was true that you have no choice but to make your fortune through a woman.'

'Through Miss Arabella Mellowes, to whom I was then supposed to be addressing myself.'

'But Miss Mellowes was not in fact to provide your fortune; you intended quite otherwise.' She said, almost forgetting her own sorrows in her rising indignation: 'At least you had the decency to arrange for a protector to be here, before bringing that young girl—which had been your intention, if I hadn't intervened and tricked you—to this house of—of ill fame...'

He dropped his hand from her arm; stood before her, his head bent, crest-fallen. 'Well—it's true as you heard, that I have—that a lady has been here. What business was it of anyone's, while I had no positive pretensions elsewhere? But if you wish it, I am willing to—dispense with her now.'

'*I* wish? What do *I* care what you do with your women? I care nothing for you *or* for them, nothing whatsoever!'

His bright eye gleamed down on her now; mocking her. 'Miss Dove—you quite shock me! Such kisses—for a man you care nothing about whatsoever!'

She pulled herself together. She said stiffly: 'I dissembled. It was necessary to keep up the pretence that you were with Miss Mellowes.'

'Miss Mellowes! Miss Mellows will never kiss a man like that if she lives to be a thousand.' He grinned, wagging his head towards a closed door, further down the corridor. 'Now, my other young lady—'

She protested, outraged, almost in tears: 'You are offensive, Mr. Havering. I care nothing for her or for any other so-called lady—'

'Then you are indifferent whether she goes or stays?

For I've told you—you have but to say that I should, and I'll send her away.'

'Send her away! Do you mean that at this moment—with all these people here, with that young girl here—this woman is still in the house?'

'I've told you—I'll get rid of her. You have only to speak the word.'

'I speak the word! What have I to do with it?'

'Well, you can't both remain here,' he said, apologetically. 'That much is evident, isn't it?'

'I have no wish or intention to stay here. All I want is to go.'

'Oh, dear,' he said, disappointed. 'Don't you like my little house?'

'I care nothing for your house; nor need it matter to *you* that I am disgusted that you should so shamelessly keep this—this—'

'This woman. But you see, the trouble is that she must keep *me*. It is she whom I rely upon for my fortune.'

A thought flashed through her mind that might save for her hungry heart, some shred of respect for him. She faltered: 'If she is some—some relative—'

'No relative, no: would I keep a relative hidden away from the company? Until a year ago, I had never set eyes on her. Once I did—well, it is true that I fell in love; I think no man could do less.' He took her hand, quite kindly. 'Will you let me take you to meet her? She is not what you think: some vulgar bawd. She is truly sweet and lovely.'

She pulled her hand sharply away. 'What are you thinking of? Certainly I won't see her.'

He looked down at her, smiling. 'Miss Dove—you are jealous!'

'I? Jealous? Jealousy must imply some—some caring...'

'And do you care nothing?' He caught at her shoulders, turned her to stand facing him; looked down into her eyes with those blue, blue eyes—with that gleam that she had recognised on that very first day of their meeting, the gleam that—rogue and villain that he might be—had pierced into her soul for ever. 'You with your calm, lovely face and those trusting dove eyes of yours—come, you are incapable of duplicity! Can you look back into my eyes and swear that you care nothing?' And, while she trembled on his arm, speechless, confounded, he led her gently a few steps forward and flung open a door. 'My little grey dove—I have teased you past all forebearance! Come now and meet my lady.'

A small room, in that tiny house. A clutter of paints and paint-strippers, of brushes and scrapers and bottles and pots ... And a picture. A heavy easel; and upon it, the picture of a woman.

The picture of a woman: against a background of Italian landscape, a young woman, a beautiful woman ... A woman whose kisses might indeed have rivalled all other kisses—four hundred years ago.

'I gambled upon her all I owned in the world,' he said. 'And now at last I know her for what she is. You see where I've started the cleaning and restoration: you see the signature? She is by Raphael—by no means one of his madonnas, but by Raphael. She is a true Raphael—and she is my fortune.' And he lifted her hand as she stood beside him, trembling; and said: 'My fortune—and yours too, if you will share it with me.'

The pure, pale oval of her face was paler than ever; her hazel eyes lifted to his in wonderment. 'Do you not know,' he said, 'that I have always loved you? From that very first moment. But until I knew—until I was certain of this—' he threw out a hand to the picture—'I couldn't be sure that I should ever be able to offer you all I would wish to. And till then I dared not ...' He broke off and even he was in some little confusion. 'Until I was sure—dare I risk that this tender heart should come under that fatal charm which—we've but lately agreed—was all too easily cast over the hearts of the little heiresses of Robinstown? But now...'

But now ... Now the blue eyes looked down into hers and she lay against his breast, held there safe and close for ever. 'My little grey dove,' he said. 'My radiant dove —you are here in your nest where you belong: at last!'